EMPEROR PICKLETINE RIDES THE BUS

AN ORIGAMI YODA BOOK

Library of Congress has catalogued
the hardcover edition of this book as follows:
Angleberger, Tom, author, illustrator.
Emperor Pickletine rides the bus : an origami yoda book / Tom Angleberger.
pages cm
Summary: The seventh graders of McQuarrie Middle School and their Star Wars-inspired origami finger puppets go on a field trip to Washington, D.C., on what proves to be a very long trip full of shifting alliances, betrayals, carsickness, and sugar rushes.
ISBN 978-1-4197-0933-3 (hardback)
ISBN for this edition: 978-1-4197-1505-1
[1. Finger puppets–Fiction. 2. Origami–Fiction. 3. Eccentrics and eccentricities–Fiction. 4. Interpersonal relations–Fiction. 5. School field trips–Fiction. 6. Bus travel–Fiction. 7. Washington (D.C.)–Fiction. 8. Humorous stories.] I. Title.
PZ7.A585Emp 2014
[Fic]–dc23
2014012574

Text copyright © 2014 Tom Angleberger
Book design by Melissa J. Arnst

Printed and bound in Australia
10 9 8 7 6 5 4 3

THE ART OF BOOKS SINCE 1949

161-165 Farrington Road
London, UK EC1R 3AL
www.abramsandchronicle.co.uk

THIS BOOK IS DEDICATED TO
CECE, CHARLIE, OSCAR, TUNA, S. M.
. . . AND TO ME, TOO. AFTER ALL,
I'VE ENJOYED THIS WILD RIDE
MORE THAN ANYONE!

KELLEN (ME)   TOMMY

FiELD TRiP!

BY TOMMY

This case file is all about the field trip!

The field trip to Washington, D.C.

The field trip we've been looking forward to all year.

Must.. Test....
Must.... Test...

The field trip we lost when Principal Rabbski got obsessed with us taking Standards tests.

The field trip we fought for and won back!

The field trip that is going to be totally stooky fizz-pop waffles with plastic dinosaurs on top, as Murky would say. (Except that Murky can't go because he's a sixth grader. But

that's okay, because he got to go somewhere else.)

The field trip that just has one little problem.

Rabbski has made a No Origami rule.

(Actually, she made a bunch of rules: No cell phones or digital cameras. No public displays of affection. No sodas. No orange-colored snacks or drinks. No peanuts—due to allergies. No ORIGAMI!)

But it's the No Origami rule that we are freaking out about.

Now, some people might think, "Big deal."

But it IS a big deal.

Some people might think, "I could get through a day without origami, no problem." In fact, some people go days, weeks, months—even long, sad lifetimes—without origami.

But for us, a day without origami is frightening.

What are we going to do if we run into trouble?

Field trips are dangerous events: a whole bunch of kids crammed into a bus for four hours to get there and then four hours to get back. ANYTHING can happen.

Just ask Quavondo! He got the nickname Cheeto Hog on last year's field trip to the zoo!

On that same trip, Amy and Sara got in an argument about something before we even left the school parking lot and didn't speak to each other the entire day . . . even though they were seat partners and couldn't switch.

And Lance broke something in the zoo gift shop. And me and Kellen got lectured by a zookeeper about ABSOLUTELY NOTHING. (Well, nothing much.)

And Jen lost $15 AND a boyfriend. And Mike cried about something. And on and on.

ZOO
HOO
TEARS

That's the sort of stuff that used to happen to us ALL the time . . . before Origami Yoda came along.

Dwight first brought him to school a little

3

while after that field trip, and he started giving us all incredible advice. Even though it was too late to help most of us with our field trip problems, his advice did help Quavondo get rid of the nickname.

SARA

And he has helped us with a million things since then, from getting me an almost sort-of girlfriend to saving THIS year's field trip. And when Origami Yoda hasn't been able to help, other origami has, like Sara's Fortune Wookiee and Amy's Art2-D2 and my Foldy-Wan Kenobi and so on.

Over the last year we've gotten used to getting help from our *Star Wars* origami with whatever problems we run into.

And now we have to leave Origami Yoda and everybody else behind?

"WUG!"

"NOOOOOOOO!"

"I have a bad feeling about this!"

SAD WHISTLE!

"I like nuts!"

We've begged Rabbski to change her mind. She's pretty friendly nowadays and you can actually talk to her about stuff. But talking to her about this does no good at all.

"I'm sorry, but this is my last field trip as a principal and I am just not going to parade you kids through our nation's capital with paper puppets on your fingers, yelling, 'May the Force be with you' at the White House. You're representing this school and . . ."

For some reason, anytime an adult decides you are "representing" something, they decide you should represent it by being as quiet and boring as possible. (I do have to admit, though, that she was right about us yelling, "May the Force be with you" at the White House. I can totally see Lance doing that.)

So this case file is about how and/or if we survive our field trip without any origami . . . not even Origami Yoda.

Rabbski may be nicer, but she's also gotten smarter.

See, I wasn't worried about the No Origami rule because I was planning to bring my new KIRIGAMI General Grievous. (Which is amazing, by the way.)

But then, right after telling Tommy for the tenth time that no origami was allowed, she looked right at me and said, "No KIRIGAMI, either."

Tommy's Comment: Yeah, she's tough these days. You'd think that since she decided to stop being a principal, she'd relax a bit. But maybe she's just trying to get it out of her system. I sure hope she does before she becomes our new math teacher next year. (By the way, the rumor is that Mr. Randall is going to be the principal when Rabbski is done! Which would be awesome! There's another rumor that says Mr. Howell will, but that's too horrible to even think about.)

OH YEAH? WELL, I DIDN'T WANT TO GO ON THE CRUMMY FIELD TRIP ANYWAY!!

ORIGAMI YODA AND THE BUS BUDDY

BY TOMMY

This is a secret chapter. I can't put it in the case file because that would be extremely rude to a certain person. But it IS an important chapter to have because, as Origami Yoda said:

"Fate of the field trip rest on this will . . ."

He said this one morning in homeroom about a week before the field trip.

I didn't like the ominous sound of his voice.

Miss Bauer just didn't like hearing his voice at all.

"Dwight, could you turn around, put away the puppet, and listen, please?" she asked, although of course she wasn't actually asking. "I need everybody to listen closely so I only have to explain this once. Here's how the seating arrangements are going to work on the field trip."

I snapped to attention. Origami Yoda was right! This was going to be a big deal. Seating arrangements can make or break a field trip, but they are a VERY delicate and tricky business. (Trickier than I knew, it turned out.)

"Have Foldy-Wan, do you?" Origami Yoda said.

"DWIGHT! I just asked you to turn around and to PUT. AWAY. THE PUPPET! I am not going to ask again!"

I did have Foldy-Wan, but stupidly didn't ask him for advice. I didn't think I needed it. Guess what? I needed it. BAD.

Miss Bauer told us about choosing our seat partners. But before I tell you what she

said, I need to warn you: It unfortunately
involves repeated use of the word "buddy."

"The field trip will work on the buddy
system," said Miss Bauer. "You'll sit with
your buddy on the bus and stick together all
day, keeping an eye out for each other."

"Wisely you must choose," Origami Yoda
told me.

"DWIGHT! Okay, you're going to ISS for the
rest of homeroom. Take your slip . . ."

Dwight took the slip and was already
folding it into something before he went out
the door. We had witnessed this scene so
many times that it seemed like a normal part
of homeroom. For a while Dwight had been
terrified of getting into trouble. But ever
since the success of the Rebellion, he had
gone back to his old ways of basically doing
whatever popped into his head.

"Now, as I was saying. You'll choose a seat
buddy, and then you and your buddy will sign
up for a 'buddy bunch,' based on which museum

you want to explore. So definitely choose a 'buddy' and a 'buddy bunch' that share your interests!

"Okay, you may talk quietly among yourselves about this until the bell."

Immediately, an earsplitting roar rose from the class.

"QUIETLY!!!!!!" yelled Miss Bauer.

Kellen turned to me and said, "Air and Space Museum, right?"

"Er . . . ," I said. This was a bit awkward.

I hadn't been prepared for this. I didn't realize we were going to have to make a decision right then. I don't mean the museum decision—that's obvious—I mean a seat "buddy" decision.

Going to Washington, D.C., with Kellen would be a lot of fun. But going with Sara . . . That could be fun and maybe more than fun. We have never had a chance to hang around together for a whole day without one of our parents—usually her mom—also hanging around. And even that has only happened a few times.

This just seemed like the perfect chance to have fun and also sort of . . . make things official between us. And, as long as this is a secret chapter, I might as well say it . . . I could sort of imagine that, after a fun day, as the bus got dark, we might actually . . . well, you know . . . It's hard to write even in a secret chapter. But maybe, maybe we would have . . . our first kiss. That would definitely make things official. And it would make it the best day ever and all that.

But . . . was I going to have to hurt Kellen's feelings to do that?

"I guess I was thinking about asking Sara," I said.

But Kellen wasn't as mad as I thought.

"Oh . . . yeah . . . that's stooky. I mean, I would drop you like a hot mynock if Rhondella would sit with me. In fact, I would ask her if I thought there was any chance she'd say yes."

"The odds are approximately ten kamillion to one," said Lance with his C-3PO.

"Never tell me the odds," said Kellen. "They're too depressing . . ."

Well, that made me feel bad for ditching Kellen, and I guess maybe Lance felt bad for Kellen, too, since the odds were 100 percent that he would be sitting with Amy.

But . . . the next period was LEGO robots class, which I have with Sara. So I took my chance. Although I wasn't thinking of it as a chance. I was assuming my odds were about 100 percent, too.

They weren't.

"Er . . . ," she said.

And I instantly realized that she had the same problem that I had just had with Kellen—not that that made me feel any better.

"You're going to go with Rhondella, aren't you?"

"You understand, right, Tommy? I mean, Rhondella is . . . well, she's . . . I can't explain it. She's been hanging out with her boyfriend so much this year. And since he's an eighth grader, he won't be on the trip, so this is my chance to do something with her again."

"All right," I muttered.

"I'll make it up to you!"

"How?"

"I'll think of something!" she said.

Well, that sounded promising, but it didn't do me any good right then.

In between classes, I rushed to Kellen's locker to see if he was there. But he wasn't, of course, since his locker is practically unusable due to being crammed with so much junk that he usually just hauls all his books around in his enormous book bag.

So, when I finally saw him in social studies, it was too late.

"Sorry, dude, Dwight and I are going to ride together. We're working on a new how-to-do-stuff case file."

"Yeah, we're going to—" And Dwight started explaining all these details about some weird variation on some doodlegami they were making. I'm sure it was awesome, but this wasn't the time for that!

"Uh, great," I said, "but who am I going to go with? Do you know if Mike signed up with anyone?"

"Yes . . . signed up everyone has," said Origami Yoda. "Everyone except . . ."

"Bom bom bom bom ba bom bom ba bom," finished Kellen.

"You don't mean—"

"Yes . . . ," said Origami Yoda. "To ride with Harvey . . . it is your destiny!"

So, at lunch, I asked him and tried to seem as happy about it as possible.

He said yes, but didn't even try to seem happy about it.

"Sara turned you down?" he asked.

"Yes."

"Ha . . . ha . . . !" he said slowly and nastily.

Whee! It's gonna be a fun trip!

My Comment: Frankly, Harvey was so rude, I'm not sure why I'm keeping this chapter a secret. Sometimes it seems like we hold back a lot to keep from hurting his feelings, and he never holds back anything.

MARA JADE HELPS REMI FIND TRUE LOVE!

BY REMI

tommy this time its okay if you put this in the case file i dont care if kellen reads it i am tired of caring about what kellen thinks

oh i didnt mean it to sound that harsh kellen im sorry and in a way im sorry about what happened but not really not at all actually but none of it is to hurt your feelings

so the first thing that happened was that i decided not to go on our field trip

the sixth grade goes to the north carolina zoological park as you know because that is where

you guys went last year and quavondo ate all the cheetos

so why would i decide not to go to a zoo especially the nc zoo which i always wanted to go to because they have a jungle house where you actually walk through the jungle?????

because kellen wouldnt be there so it would be a whole day without seeing kellen AND worrying that rhondella was making a move on him back at school

YOU DIDN'T NEED TO WORRY!

so i decided i wouldnt go . . . if you dont go on the trip you get to stay at school and "work" in the library all day i knew it wouldnt be so bad since mrs calhoun always lets me make stuff from craft books PLUS i would get to see kellen every time he came into the library and i could go to the seventh-grade lunch period and actually sit at the rebellion table with all of the rest of you for the first time!!!

awesome idea!!!

then i told mara jade about my idea

"your skull must be thicker than a blast shield!"

she was pretty serious about it she also used
some soapy the monkey language

H@W!

but i still wasnt sure

i asked wicket and he shouted at me

"KVARK! X'iutha treekthin!"

but i still wasnt sure

so i asked origami yoda

"hrrmmmm . . ." he said "if here you stay nothing
will change but field trips everything can change . . .
like soap opera on a bus they are"

Well when mara wicket and yoda all agree then
you got to listen

i decided to go on the trip and when it was time
to sign up for bus buddies i figured i would ask
megan (the one who calls herself fred) but then
ben asked me first

BEN

normally the ony thing we do together is make
origami but as you know rabbski doesnt allow origami
on field trips but we figured we could get away
with folding some stuff on the bus

but we were wrong but i'll let murky tell you
about that part

because the important part to me is what ben and i did after rabbski took away our origami paper

first we talked and goofed around then walked through the zoo and fell in love and held hands and kissed in the jungle house in front of the meerkats until mr howell yelled at us

on the way home i said maybe it wasnt right for me to fall in love with ben when my character is mara jade and her true love is luke skywalker which kellen made

and ben said "i can make a better luke skywalker than kellen" and he very very quietly folded up some brochure that he had picked up at the otter playground into an AMAZING STOOKY FIZZ-POP luke skywalker

sorry kellen but it IS a lot better than yours

and now we are together forever and thank you mara jade and wicket and origami yoda . . . and sorry kellen

CAUTION LOOSE GORILLA STILL LOOSE!

YEAH . . . RIGHT.

Harvey's Comment

Can we please keep kissing out of the case files? (And Mara Jade, too?)

WATCH IT, PUNK!

OR I'LL FORCE CHOKE YOUR FACE!

19

My Comment: I was a little worried about showing this chapter to Kellen even though Remi said I could. I was worried it would hurt his feelings or make him regret not paying more attention to Remi when she still liked him.

But when I told him about it, he said, "Huh?"

"Remi! The girl who's been chasing you all year!"

"She has?"

"Well, not anymore."

"Oh, okay."

I'm afraid the poor dude is still stuck on Rhondella. But maybe OUR field trip will change things for him.

I GOT TO AGREE WITH HARVEY... NO MORE KISSING!

YEAH, THAT WAS GROSS!

BUT SHE DID HAVE COOL ARM SOCKS!!!

MONTDALE HOT DOG CO. HAT

PINK SHIRT

MURKY

BOO-HOO AT THE ZOO-HOO

BY MURKY

Pikpok Pete!!!!!!!!!!

zoo trip was so nostrul.

how nostrul? well we saw a hippo that had a gallon of snot coming out of its nostril. it was a really big nostril but this trip was twice as nostrul as that nostril.

people, it's three and a half hours to the zoo from school. that's seven hours on a bus and no video games no music no tv.

it is the perfect time to do origami because what else are you going to do?

THE MINCH

1ST PERSON TO EVER WEAR A ~~CUMBERBUND~~ TO THE ZOO — CUMMERBUND

my "bus buddy" Adam Minch and I were folding before the bus even left the parking lot

and Rabbski was yelling her narnar at us before we even left the parking lot!

"didn't you read the permission slip? didn't you read the rules? didn't you see the no origami rule?"

of course I didn't read the rules who reads the rules????????

QUI-GON??

so we gave her the stuff we were working on. I had been halfway thru a totally triangular Qui-Gon Jinn!

so we waited for her to sit down and then got more paper out of our backpacks

suddenly she's there glaring at us again and she took the rest of our paper

isn't the rule that you should remain seated when the bus is in motion more important than a no origami rule???

anyway here's the whole trip: narnar, narnar, narnar, <u>hippo snot</u>, red monkey

22

bottoms, narnar, narnar, narnar, back at school, the end.

Harvey's Comment

Ha! I knew you were fools to think Rabbski was your principAL all of a sudden! Like I said, she's just as Sith-like as ever.

By the way, have the sixth-grade teachers stopped teaching grammar? Having Murky and Remi files next to each other is just too much! You should have deleted both of them!

My Comment: Uh, yeah . . . . I think that's maybe a tiny bit harsh, Harvey.

Murky's file is especially important because it shows that Rabbski means business with her No Origami rule. I was hoping she wouldn't actually bother to enforce it. But it sounds like she is totally serious about it.

As I've said before, the prospect of a No Origami field trip was pretty wug. Especially since the bus buddy thing was already a disaster.

But then Kellen had an idea . . .

YOU SAID IT, CHEWIE! THIS BUS IS SO SLOW IT DOES THE KESSEL RUN IN 12,349,624,532,710,922 PARSECS!

23

$$(S+R) - (S+T) = R+K!$$

"Sara being bus buddies with Rhondella is the best thing that could have happened," he said.

"If Rhondella had gone with Jen, there is NO WAY they would have been in our buddy bunch. BUT if you can get Sara and Rhondella to join our buddy bunch, then you get to spend the whole day with Sara and I get to spend the whole day with Rhondella!"

A New Hope!

Like Yoda said, it COULD change everything!

"As Murky would say, 'Shakespearean!'" I said.

"Actually, I think he would be more likely to call this one 'SlickSlack!'" said Kellen.

"Well, whatever. Let's see if it works!"

It didn't.

I'M SO GLAD YOU'RE MY BUS BUDDY!

UH . . . YEAH . . . COULD YOU MAYBE STOP JIGGLING?

THE BIG PINK

WILLY THE SITTING WAFFLE

CASSIE

NOBODY WANTS TO PEE ON THE BUS

BY CASSIE

When Rabbski announced that we were going to get to go on our big field trip after all, everybody was excited ... except me.

I would have been happy to go to Greenhill Plantation, which is, like, ten minutes away. — HOPEFULLY!

A ten-minute field trip doesn't require peeing on a bus.

But when you take a big field trip, they rent these giant buses that have a toilet in the back. And if you have to go to the bathroom, you walk back there, go in the tiny room, and pee in a teensy toilet.

Except I can't.

TOILET

BUS

DRAWN
EXACTLY
TO SCALE

I don't want to go into a lot of detail here, but basically I need a little peace and quiet to pee. It's not just that I prefer it that way, it's that I actually cannot pee when there is either hubbub or stress.

What's stressful about using a bus bathroom? Oh, nothing, except that everybody on the bus sees you go in there! And when you sit there you wonder if they are thinking about you using the bathroom. And then you wonder if they are timing you. Not with a watch or anything. But when you come out, is someone going to think, "Man, she sure was in there a long time"? And that makes it harder to pee, which means that it's taking even longer, which means that it really is a long time!

And the whole time you're thinking about all this, the bus is rocking back and forth and hitting bumps and you're flopping all over and the nasty used water is sloshing around underneath you!!!!!!

I know all of this because last year when we went to the zoo, I tried to hold it as long as I could, but I had to go SO bad that I finally went back there. And it was terrible and tiny and gross. And I sat there forever and couldn't go! So I came out and went back to my seat

and had to sit there about to explode until we got to the zoo! Never again!

It turns out I'm not the only one!

I told Sara and Rhondella what I was worried about and they had their own problems!

"Last year?" said Rhondella. "I was sitting in the front of the bus? So when I got up to go back to the bathroom, I had to pass EVERY SINGLE PERSON on the bus? And they all know why you're going back there, too!"

"The worst thing of all," said Sara, "is worrying that someone is out there waiting to use it. And somehow it's the one person on the bus that didn't see you go back there. So instead of waiting, they keep pulling on the door. And any second the latch is going to come loose and the door is going to open and everybody is going to see you sitting on the tiny toilet."

We asked some more people:

Lisa: The walls are so thin! What if someone hears you?

Piper: And the boys pee all over the seat!

Hannah: And remember how Harvey sat back there on

DOOR LATCH

ONE MM OF PLASTIC IS ONLY THING HOLDING DOOR SHUT!

the zoo trip and said, "Hope everything comes out okay" to everybody who had to go?

Jen: And if you're the one waiting, you have to stand back there getting bumped around for ten minutes, making small talk with whoever is sitting back there, and pretending you aren't about to bust.

Amy: And what if you ARE the person who is sitting back there next to the toilet! Smells, noises . . . some field trip.

I asked Sara's Fortune Wookiee about it, but all he would say was "Wug." And all Han Foldo would say was "I don't care what you smell! Get in there!"

None of the other puppets did much good. R2-D2 doesn't have to pee. Ventress doesn't give a ding-dang what anybody thinks about her. And my puppet, Sy Snootles, doesn't do anything but sing "Call Me Maybe" in pig Latin.

So, Sara said we should ask Origami Yoda.

"Oh, man, he's just going to tell me to ask Sherlock Dwight and then Dwight will flop around pretending to

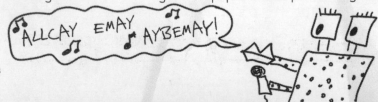

ALLCAY EMAY AYBEMAY!

smoke a pipe and yell, 'Elementary, dear Cassie' in a terrible British accent."

"Gotta do it," said Sara.

So I did.

Origami Yoda told me to ask Sherlock Dwight, and then Dwight flopped around pretending to smoke a pipe and yelled, "Elementary, dear Cassie" in a terrible British accent.

Then he said, "Consider this: The standard charter bus carries fifty-four passengers. That's room for forty-eight students and six chaperones. The number of students in our grade is two hundred twenty. Two hundred twenty divided by forty-eight is about four-point-five. That is four-and-a-half bus-fuls."

1/2 BUS →

"Uh-huh," I said.

"Now, renting a bus is expensive. So, will they actually pay for a big bus and then only have it half full?"

"Uh . . . no?"

"Of course they won't! They will add one regular school bus. Probably one of the older buses because they are smaller, but that I cannot say for certain. Anywhat, regular school buses do not have a bathroom, so logically

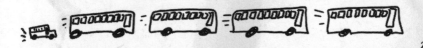

the school bus will have to stop for at least one bathroom break at a rest stop on the way to Washington, D.C."

"Awesome! How do I get on that bus?"

"Elem—"

"Never mind. I'll figure it out for myself."

But I couldn't figure it out. So I had to go back and ask Sherlock Dwight again.

"Tell me, but please don't say 'elementary.'"

"But, of course, dear lady," said Sherlock Dwight. "Students don't get to pick which bus they ride on— but chaperones do. You simply need to sign up with a chaperone who will also choose the regular bus."

"How do I know which—"

"Elementary!"

"One of these days, Dwight, I am going to—"

"Stop right there. You don't want to run afoul of this school's zero tolerance policy on threats of violence. I made that mistake once myself, causing all sorts of rannygazoo."

"Rannygazoo?"

"Yes, I say, it was a real rannygazoo!"

"Okay . . . Could you just tell me which chaperone it is elementary for me to pick?"

"Consider this . . . If you're embarrassed to go to the bathroom on the bus, think how Ms. Rabbski must feel! A principal rules by fear and respect . . . but it's hard to fear or respect someone once you've seen them cram into the tiny bus toilet to pee . . . or noticed that they were taking too long just to pee!

"But Ms. Rabbski is a veteran of many field trips. She knows to take the regular bus. And—as the principal—she has the authority to whisper in the bus driver's ear and have the bus make an unscheduled stop if necessary! If you ride the regular bus, you may actually get two or three stops on the way!"

I explained this to the other girls and we decided to join together to make a "buddy bunch"—dumb name—and ask Ms. Rabbski to be our chaperone. (Except for Amy, who is going to ride with Lance and whatever buddy bunch of potty-seat-peeing-on boys he rides with. She thinks she can hold it.)

Harvey's Comment

This is a clever plan. But it's not worth it. I mean, compare: Riding on a charter bus with air-conditioning

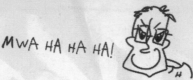

MWA HA HA HA!

and comfy seats . . . or riding on a cruddy school bus like we already ride on every single day? Plus, how are you going to have any fun with Rabbski yelling at you all the time?

Hmmm . . . in fact, this gives me a great idea!

My Comment: I really, really don't like the sound of that! Harvey's great ideas usually end up being great big pains in the behind!

The problem for me with the girls' plan is that now it looks like I'm not even going to be on the same bus as Sara!!!! I tried to talk Kellen into joining a "buddy bunch" on the regular bus, but he said Luke Skyfolder said we should ask Origami Yoda first.

Origami Yoda said, "Howell that bus will ride, too!"

I don't know how that's possible, since Mr. Howell is a sixth-grade teacher, but if Origami Yoda says so, it must be true.

And Kellen said he would rather find out his father is Darth Vader, have his hand cut off, and fall into a giant air conditioner . . . than ride on Howell's bus.

WELCOME ABOARD, LADIES!

I'VE GOT A BAD FEELING
ABOUT THIS . . .

BY SARA

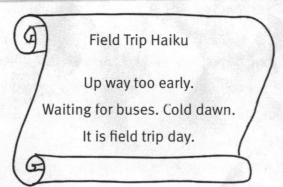

Field Trip Haiku

Up way too early.
Waiting for buses. Cold dawn.
It is field trip day.

Dwight's mom dropped us off at school. There was already a huge crowd.

It was chaos.

Rabbski was trying to line people up for buses and into buddy bunches and assign chaperones. And it was especially hard since the buses weren't there yet.

ACTUAL
PHOTO OF
RHONDELLA'S
BOYFRIEND →

JABBA
NO
BADDA!

It was freezing, but also exciting. It was going to be awesome to have an adventure with Rhondella and WITHOUT her boyfriend.

But then that didn't happen. He was THERE even though he wasn't there, if you know what I mean.

She kept trying to text him. And since cell phones were against the rules, she was making a big production out of doing it secretly by hiding the phone in her shirtsleeve, then taking it out, then hiding it, then taking it out, etc.

"Why isn't he writing back?" she whined.

"Uh, maybe because it's six in the morning and he isn't even up yet!"

"Aw . . . he's sleeping! I bet he is so cute when he's sleeping! And then he'll get up with his hair all mussy! I'm going to ask him to send a selfie the second he wakes up!"

I didn't have the Fortune Wookiee and Han Foldo with me, but I knew what they would be saying: "WUG" and "I have a bad feeling about this."

But what I really needed was their advice! Because spending the whole day watching Rhondella send selfies back and forth with her boyfriend was not what I had planned!

"Maybe it wouldn't be too late to switch," I thought . . .

But right then Ms. Rabbski started yelling on the bullhorn again:

"I need my group and Mr. Howell's group and Mrs. Porterfield's group to go ahead and load up on the yellow bus. NOW!"

I couldn't believe it! What Origami Yoda had told Tommy was right: For whatever reason, Howell was going on the field trip and . . . we'd be on his bus ALL day!

I waved good-bye to Tommy. He looked pretty sad. Harvey was standing next to him, complaining his head off about something already.

Just as we were getting on the regular bus, the REAL buses showed up.

Bus Haiku
by Sara

Big buses roll in
Roomy and magnificent!
Ours is so small. Wug.

OK . . . ENOUGH WITH THE "WUG" ALREADY . . .

"Climb aboard, ladies! Quickly!" said Ms. Rabbski.

The stress of lining everyone up and confiscating origami paper from Kellen, Tommy, and Dwight had completely worn away the niceness she had been showing since the school board meeting.

"We're going to get a head start on those other buses," she barked. "They're a little bit faster . . . Plus, we may make a rest stop or two on the way . . . So stow yourself and get settled and no silly business. I'll review the rules once we're under way."

"And I may add a few rules of my own," said Mr. Howell.

We walked back to our seats. The same boring, uncomfortable bus seats we always sit on. In fact, as I sat down I realized this WAS the same bus I ride every day. I recognized the patterns of chipped, scratched paint and the smell of despair . . .

Was this worth it just to have a nicer bathroom? That would have been two minutes of embarrassment . . . but this was starting to seem like a whole day in the Sarlacc Pit.

Well, how do you think I feel? I have to use the boys' bathroom all the time! So I have to face the horror and indignity of peed-upon-seats every day of my life because of slobs like Tommy!

My Comment: WHAT????? Why are you blaming me for peeing on toilet seats! I don't pee on the seats! I have never peed on a seat! Do you have any idea how strict my mother is about lifting the seat before you pee and then putting it back down again? Next to "NO DRINKS IN THE LIVING ROOM" it's her number one rule.

So, Sara, or any other girls who end up reading this case file . . . it's not me!

DARTH MAUL'S GUIDE TO NOT PEEING ON THE SEAT!

1. GET A BIT OF T.P.

2. USE T.P. TO LIFT SEAT

3. TOSS T.P. IN COMMODE . . .

4. READY . . . * AIM . . . SINK THE T.P.!

5. USE A NEW PIECE OF T.P. TO FLUSH, THEN LOWER LID.

AND DON'T FORGET TO WASH YOUR HANDS, FOR CRYING OUT LOUD!!!

I'VE GOT AN EVEN BADDER FEELING ABOUT THIS!

BY AMY

What was I thinking? I should have made Lance join Sara's bus buddy group, instead of me going with his!

Here's the rest of the group: Tommy and Harvey, Dwight and Kellen, Mike and Quavondo! (Kellen, please draw a seating chart.)

Yeesh! These boys are louder than you could possibly imagine!!!

They were quiet while Rabbski was still here, because she came over and yelled at them first thing. Then she actually searched their backpacks

SODA   PAPER CLIP CATAPULT   GOOGLY EYES   RUBBER BAND BALL   CONFISCATED!

SEATING CHART

for origami paper and toys. She even searched mine!

She took everything we had that was made of paper, including Mike's Holocron Notebook. (He almost cried!)

I begged her not to take my journal (which has some very personal information in it). Luckily, she let me keep it—which is how I have paper to write this right now—but she made me promise not to tear sheets out of it since the boys would make origami with them.

I told her, "Don't worry. The last thing I want is to have them making puppets and doing Star Wars impressions all day!"

So the minute she got on the regular bus and drove away, they got loud and they've been that way ever since!

You'd think our chaperone would make them be quiet, but you WILL NOT BELIEVE who our chaperone is . . .

Mr. Good Clean Fun.
AND SOAPY!!!

DID YOU MISS ME?

HOLO CRON

Yes, that's right, he brought Soapy!!!!

And while other chaperones were reciting rules like "Stay calm," "No yelling," and stuff like that, Mr. Good Clean Fun was saying stuff like:

"Don't bring home germs as a souvenir!"

He didn't have any real rules, like "Don't bug Amy." Not that I want to go on a field trip with a drill sergeant, but that would be better than this herd of lawless boys.

Everything they do turns into insanity.

Like, before we left, the bus driver, C.J., opened up a big door on the side of the bus and pulled out these enormous coolers to hold our lunches.

Okay, so you just line up and put your lunch in the cooler, right? Oh, no, the boys were pushing and shoving and throwing stuff. I didn't want to get involved so I asked Lance to put my lunch in . . . and Harvey knocked it out of his hand and pretended he was going to sit on it . . . but then someone pushed him and he lost his balance and actually DID sit on it!

SANDWICH

HARVEY'S BEHIND

PLASTIC BAG (NOT ZIPLOC)

THE MARK OF THE HARVEY!

So now I have a turkey sandwich with Harvey's butt print on it to look forward to at lunch!

When we got on the bus, Mr. Good Clean Fun held up an enormous backpack.

"I've brought two types of hand sanitizer—gels and wipes. No need to be stingy with it—I brought plenty! In fact, let's start this trip on the right foot by starting with clean hands!"

Then he went down the aisle, squirting everybody, even people in other groups.

"Okay, now I'm just going to slip back and wipe down the bathroom for everyone! And I'll be sitting right back there next to the potty to give you a fresh squirt of sanitizer after you use it."

"A little squirt never hurt anything but dirt," screeched Soapy.

Thus began the reign of lawlessness. The other chaperones were sitting in the front of the bus and only turned around to try to hush the boys once, when we passed Greenhill Plantation and they all started yelling and blowing raspberries.

PBBLLLLTHHHHHH!

THAT WAS HURTFUL!

COW POO

(MOO-HOO TEARS)

I just want to say that I thought it was Lance's lunch and I would never have done that to your lunch, Amy. I apologize.

My Comment: MMMMMM . . . HarveyButtWich! A lunchtime favorite! Choose Regular or Extra Spicy!!

KELLEN

PICKLE STINK

(ME)

THE DARK SIDE IS STRONG ON THIS BUS . . . AND SO IS THE SMELL OF PICKLE

BY KELLEN

As usual, this case file would be a total disaster without me! See, even though Rabbski took away Tommy's notebook and Mike's Holocron—which is also a notebook—she didn't take my brother's recorder thingy, which looks basically like a key chain.

I knew I couldn't record the whole trip—and who would want to?—but I kept it handy in case something unusual happened.

So, naturally, when Tommy said, "Gross, Harvey! Did you just pull that out of your underwear?" I hit the REC button right away.

So, here's what happened after Tommy said, "Gross, Harvey! Did you just pull that out of your underwear?"

Harvey: [Evil chuckle.]

Tommy: Whut the Hutt is that?

Harvey: Heh heh heh heh . . . It has all happened as I have foreseen . . .

[It was Harvey doing a voice like a dying cow with a British accent.]

Tommy: Get it out of my face. Hey! I'm serious! It stinks!

[Harvey was looking so freakishly pleased with himself that I wanted to punch him even before I figured out what he was up to. When I did figure it out, I REALLY wanted to punch him!

He had an origami puppet on his finger. All black. It was like a black robe with a hood. And inside the hood was . . . a pickle. Actually, a wrinkly, nasty pickle slice with a couple of mean-looking red eyeballs stuck on.]   HEH HEH HEH . . .

Mike: [Leaning over the back of the seat.]
          Is that Emperor Palpatine?
Harvey: No . . . It's . . .
[He took a long pause, enjoying the fact that
he had an audience. I wish I hadn't given him
the pleasure of seeing me watch him in his
moment of triumph. But how could you NOT look?]
Harvey: It's Emperor PICKLEtine!
Tommy: Is that a real pickle? No wonder it
          stinks . . .
Pickletine: Behold the power of the Sour Side
          of the Force!
Mike: Uh, Harvey? Maybe you didn't notice
          the fifty times she said it, but Ms.
          Rabbski has banned origami on the
          field trip!
Pickletine: That may be so . . . But tell me . . .
          where is your Ms. Rabbski now?
Mike: She's on another bus.
Pickletine: Yes . . . Yes . . . it is just as I
          have foreseen . . . She is on another
          bus . . . And I am on THIS one! Heh

heh heh . . . You pathetic rule-followers have given up your Lukes and your Obi-Wans and even your Yodas. You don't even have any of your precious little origami papers . . . And now I AM THE ULTIMATE POWER ON THIS BUS!

Quavondo: [Next to Mike, also peeking over the seat back.] What if we tell, uh, Mr. Good Clean Fun?

Pickletine: Oh . . . Do you think that little man will help you?

[Even listening to the recording, the croaky smugness of Pickletine's voice is infuriating! Especially since he was right. At that moment, Mr. Good Clean Fun was passing out little packs of Kleenex to everyone. Well, actually, Soapy was the one passing them out.]

Soapy: The boogers on the bus go in the Kleenex, in the Kleenex, in the Kleenex . . .

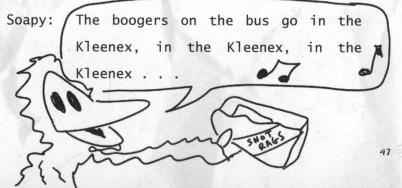

Kellen: Okay, fine, but what if I tell Miss Bauer?

Pickletine: Yes . . . Yes . . . Go right ahead. Turn in another student for making origami. Yes . . . Give in to your feelings! Tell on me! Strike me down! And once you tattle, your journey to the Sour Side will be complete."

Lance: He's right. It would be pretty unstooky to tattle on him.

Me (Kellen): So we've got to listen to the Emperor gripe at us all day?

Mike: Yeah, and what if . . . you know . . . the pickle has . . . powers?

Lance: Powers?

Mike: Yeah, powers. Like Origami Yoda. What if Pickletine can use the Sour Side to make our whole field trip miserable?

Me (Kellen): He's already doing that! I've been miserable since Harvey brought

PICKLE POWERS?

48

him out. And Tommy's right. It DOES stink!

Mike: Wait a minute . . . Dwight! Dwight! Dude! Any chance you snuck Origami Yoda on board? Hopefully not in your underwear.

Dwight: No, I left him at home . . . but . . . he did warn me that this might happen.

Tommy: Really? What did he tell you to do?

Dwight: He said, "Fruit Roll-Ups you must bring," so I brought a whole bagful. Lime.

[He opened up a big brown paper bag. A sack, really.]

Me (Kellen): Woah, dude! That is a LOT of Fruit Roll-Ups.

Tommy: But that doesn't do us any good!

Me (Kellen): Yeah, especially since I hate lime . . .

Pickletine: Heh heh heh . . . Yes, just as I had foreseen!

Lance: You foresaw that Kellen hates lime
           Fruit Roll-Ups?

Pickletine: No, you fool! I foresaw that your
            insignificant Origami Yoda and his
            stupid advice would be useless! Now,
            prepare to witness—

Me (Kellen): Wait a minute, Tickletine! I
             think YOU need to witness THIS!

Lance: Amy! Check it out!!!

Amy: What is it? [I couldn't see her, but
           it sounded like she was rolling her
           eyes.]

Lance: Dwight's folding a Fruit Roll-Up!

Amy: It just gets worse and worse . . .

[But the rest of us all had our eyes
glued on Dwight and his Fruit Roll-Up. He
had finished folding it—it was a five-fold
emergency Yoda—and was sticking it on his
finger.]

Dwight: Fruitigami Yoda I am. Guide you I
           will.

Kellen: YES! In your face, Harvey!

Voice of Authority: Is there a problem here?

[It was Miss Bauer!]

Miss Bauer: Lance, Mike, and Quavondo, I need you to sit on your bottoms and face forward. Kellen, you need to keep your voice down. And Dwight, I see you are already eating. Well . . . Okay . . . I guess it's okay for you all to start on your snacks. But go slow, they need to last you all the way to Washington. AND KEEP THE NOISE DOWN. You have been WAY too loud already!

[A bunch of other kids wanted to know if they could eat their snacks, too, so Miss Bauer went back to the front of the bus and made an announcement about it. Then Mr. Good Clean Fun ran up to the front and yelled: "Don't snack on germs!!!!" And he started squirting sanitizer on everybody again.]

Me (Kellen): Uh, Dwight. Did you just eat Fruitigami Yoda?

Dwight: [Gulps.] That's why I brought so many Fruit Roll-Ups. I can make a new one whenever we need it. See?

[And he made another one.]

Fruitigami Yoda II: Return I will . . . Help you fight the Sour Side I will.

[Then he ate that one, too.]

Lance: [Turning around again.] How did you hide Pickletine from Miss Bauer, Harvey? Did you eat him, too?

Tommy: No. He shoved it back in his underpants.

Harvey's Comment

Just to be clear: Pickletine (a) is awesome, (b) requires some serious folding to make the robe, (c) actually looks like Palpatine because the pickle part looks all wrinkly, and (d) has evil eyes made from Red Hots candies.

Meanwhile, fruitigami Yoda is (a) lousy origami that (b) doesn't have arms, eyes, or even a face, and (c) looks even more like a big booger than Paperwad Yoda.

And most importantly:

At no point did Pickletine come in contact with my underpants. I hid him inside my hooded sweatshirt, not in my pants!

My Comment: I saw what I saw.

FRENZY!

BY TOMMY, KELLEN, MIKE, LANCE, AND QUAVONDO

Right after what happened in the last file happened, this happened:

Dwight made ANOTHER Fruitigami Yoda.

It said: "Oh, yeah . . . make stuff from snacks should you, too!"

The frenzy began!

Everybody started digging in their snack bags to see what they had brought and what they could make.

We made some semi-cool stuff—which will show up in the next file—but we had more ideas

than actual food. So Kellen has drawn the
ones we couldn't make . . .

CORN TROOPER

TUSKEN TATER

DARTH MAULSHMALLOW

CROUTON-TAUN

C3P YOLK

VAIDER AID

POTATO WEDGE ANTILLES

TEA VIZLA

R2 T2

TEAK-421

MANGO LORIAN

A-SODA TANO

JUICE BOXXA

BANANA FETT

BOBA FRUIT

THIS IS BREAD FIVE! I'M GOING IN!

MANGO FETT

OBI WAN BALONEY

SALACIOUS -GUM-

CABBAGE OPPRESS

WATTOMELON

A NAPKIN SKYWALKER

GENERAL GRAVYUS

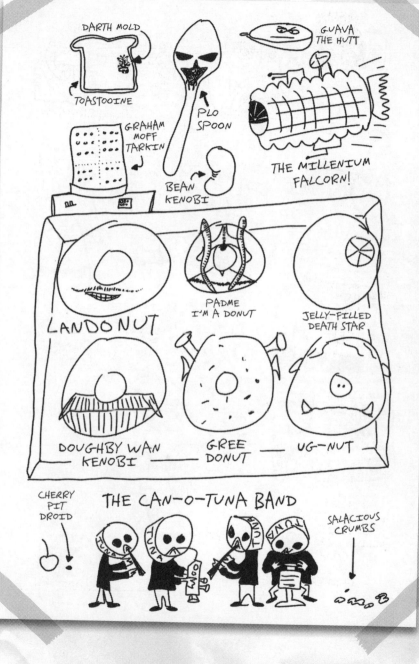

CHIP FISTO

KIT CHIPSO

CHIP CHIPSO?

DIP FORTUNA

JABBA THE GUAC

JAW-A-BREAKER

CAUTION: NEVER ORDER 66 SCOOPS!!!

CONE TROOPER

HAMMOREAN GUARD

CANDY CANE BANE

CHEW BAKLAVA (A GREEK DESSERT)

FRUIT PIE-WALKER

ORANGE MARMA JADE

JAR JAR

CHEW BROCCOLI

OLIVE YOUS
WITH I PIMENTNOS

NIEN CRUMB

QUI-GON GINGERSNAP

FRY-GON JINN

CASHEW BACCA

BOWL-O FATT

LANDO CANNEDRISIAN

P E A W O K S

COD BANE

BIB FOR-TUNA

YEE HA!

HONEY DEWBACK

WILLY THE WALKING JEDI WAFFLE

GENERAL ROOT BEERS

MILLENNIUM BACON!

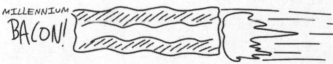

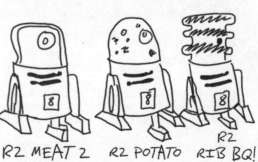

R2 TOFU

R2 MEAT 2

R2 POTATO

R2 RIB BQ!

SOMEONE SAVE ME

BY AMY

Remember what I told Rabbski? How the last thing I wanted was everybody making puppets and doing Star Wars quotes all day?

I was wrong. The really truly last thing I wanted was everybody making FOOD puppets AND doing Star Wars quotes all day.

I admit, I thought about making something, too, but all I had was a plastic baggie with some granola in it. My mom doesn't believe in junk food.

But even if I had made something, I wouldn't have been so obnoxious about it! Or so loud! These must be the loudest boys in the world!

Here's a little snapshot of my life:

Lance makes cheese robot.

Lance sticks cheese robot in my face.

Lance yells, "I am General Cheesy-us! Cower in fear, Jedi scum!"

STRING CHEESE! NICE ONE, LANCE!

And then Mike bellows across the aisle: "Luke, I am your Funyun!"

And then Kellen leans over from behind us to holler, "I am the Wheat Thinquisitor!" and part of his puppet falls off and lands in my hair!

And Harvey is yammering away nonstop with his pickle.

And then Quavondo goes, "OOH-SOME! These Goldfish look kind of like Ackbar! Commence attack on the main reactor!!!!"

Then he flicks the Goldfish with his finger and it flies across the aisle and hits me in the forehead.

"Oh, sorry, Amy!"

Apology not accepted, Admiral Dipwad!

I tried to talk to Lance about something else . . . anything else . . . but he was chomping on a whole pack of gum at once . . . (Not a good look, LanLan!)

61

LIME → RASPBERRY GRAPE

"Jubst ba mibnute," he slobbered. "I'mb gboing to bmake Bubble Fett!"

And then he did . . .

So I just looked out the window and wept silently to myself . . . The tears are streaming down my face and splattering on my journal even as I write this. (Not really, but close.)

Harvey's Comment

I agree with Amy! The behavior of the rest of you was loud, obnoxious, and embarrassing.

However, I do have to point out: General Grievous is a CYBORG, not a robot!!!!!!

My Comment: Thanks, Harvey. I'm sure that makes Amy feel much better.

Amy, on behalf of myself and the other boys: I apologize. We got carried away.

But I do have to point out that it really only lasted about half an hour. After a while, we ran out of ideas and some of us got hungry and ate the characters.

Except for Emperor Pickletine, of course. Harvey continued to stick him in MY face every chance he got.

MADE YOU LOOK!

BY MIKE

After the snacks were gone, I got up to use the bathroom. I won't go into detail here, but let's just say that the bus hit a bump right in the middle of things.

BUMP!

Then, after I get out of the bathroom, Mr. Good Clean Fun goes, "Did you wash your hands?"

"Of course!" I said.

"Did you use a paper towel when you touched the doorknob?"

"Uh . . . no . . . What . . . I mean, it was more of a latch . . . but . . . No?"

So he makes me go back into the bathroom,

KELLEN'S NOTE:
IF YOU THINK I'M DRAWING THE BATHROOM LATCH AGAIN, YOU'RE NUTS!

DON'T SAY IT!

wash my hands again, and this time use a paper towel when I open the door.

While I'm in there, he tries to make everybody sing a song about it. Actually, it was more of a rap: "Don't Touch This!"

So when I finally do come out of the bathroom (again)—using a paper towel, of course—everybody is looking at me. I think even Mace Windu would lose his cool over something like that!

But then I had an idea. Since everybody was already looking at me, this would be a great time to start a game of "Made You Look."

So, I pointed out the window and said, "Is that a hippo or a rhinoceros?"

They all looked, and I said, "Welcome to 'Made You Look,' the game show where you just looked out the window to see if an African land mammal was driving down the interstate. Winner of Round One is . . . ME!"

"Made You Look" is a game that is exactly what it says it is. Me and Cyndi played it on the RightWayKidz van trip to Joyfest and we had

THE REST OF THE RIGHTWAY KID2 AND PASTOR JJ!

more "joy" doing that than actually being at Joyfest. A LOT more!

Basically, what you do is try to get the other person or persons to look out the window at something that is not there. You get a point for everyone who looks. And they get a point if they DON'T look.

HI THERE!

You can play by shouting, "OH, NO! We're about to hit a MOOSE!!!!" Or you can be more subtle and say something like "Huh, you don't usually see a moose this far south."

"I'm afraid your pathetic attempt failed with me," said Emperor Pickletine/Harvey. "I was NOT fooled!"

"Okay," I said. He was being a jerk, but I still wanted to be fair. "Well done. You get a point for not looking."

"Oh, no," said Amy. "Please tell me we're not ACTUALLY going to play this!"

"You already ARE playing it!" I said.

"If I had Art2-D2, he would beep something really nasty at you," she said.

65

"How rude," said Lance. "I for one am most intrigued by your game. Please explain the rules."

I did.

"I made Quavondo, Lance, Amy, Tommy, and Kellen look. So I've got five. Harvey and Dwight each have one for not looking."

"The only reason Dwight didn't look was because he is trying to dig an old comb out of the bus seat," said Kellen.

"That still counts," I said.

"Uh, Mike?" asked Amy. "What happens if we really do see something out the window, like THAT!" And she pointed out the window, behind me.

I turned around to see what she was talking about. There was nothing there.

"Made you look!" said Amy.

"You may have made some of your pathetic friends look," said Pickletine, "but I can assure you that I did not . . . Oh, yes, I—"

"Can it, Pickle-breath!" said Amy. "I know I

got at least four: Mike, Quavondo, Tommy, and Kellen."

"Cattle stampede!" yelled Kellen, pointing out his window.

HIGHLY UNLIKELY

No one looked. Obviously, no one was going to get fooled again right away, although Lance and Kellen kept trying.

"Spaceship!"

"Guy popping wheelies!"

"The bus driver's asleep!"

Dwight got everybody—except Harvey—by suddenly saying, "This comb has mummified boogers on it." (It didn't, but Mr. GCF overheard and thought a used comb was disgusting anyway and made Dwight wipe his hands with two different kinds of wipes. He threw the comb into the toilet and then wiped his own hands with both kinds of wipes.)

No one ever got Harvey. He refused to look for anything. If you tried to get him, he would just look at you and wave his stinky pickle and say, "Pitiful attempt!" I decided it would be my goal to get him . . . at any cost.

Then Lance was saying, "Look, guys! It's the regular bus! We're about to pass it!!!"

I was tempted to look, but resisted.

"NO, really! Really! I'm not playing the game! You're going to miss it!"

"Hey! There's Sara!" said Amy.

I couldn't resist anymore and glanced over. The bus really was there!

We all jumped out of our seats and yelled and waved. Not just our "buddy bunch" but everybody on the bus. Obviously, the kids on the other bus couldn't hear us, but you know, it was one of those things.

"Mr. Howell is on the bus!" yelled Tommy. "And he's naked!"

I was looking for Howell during the first part of Tommy's sentence, but as soon as I heard "naked" I knew it was a part of the game and I turned away.

This started a big argument over how many points Tommy should get. Tommy claimed that Harvey glanced out the window right then, but Harvey said he was just making sure that the

people on the other bus could see the magnificence of Emperor Pickletine. (Yeah, I'm sure they were real impressed.)

This just made me more determined to get Harvey fair and square and in a way that he couldn't argue his way out of.

Also, Miss Bauer came to the back of the bus to fuss at ALL of us about the "naked" thing, even though it was Tommy that said it. Then she fussed at Mr. GCF and he promised to keep us quiet. So he started to lecture us about our behavior, but somehow it ended up being about how our bodies were changing and how we would need to start using deodorant.

Worth it. Totally worth it!

Harvey's Comment

Even if I did look—which I did not—I still won the game by a million points!

My Comment: When we passed the bus, I got to wave at Sara and she waved back, and it looked like she was

mouthing the words "I wish I was with you!" I figured
that was probably just what I wished she were saying,
but later on she told me she really was saying that,
because she was having a terrible time.

BUT! Us waving at her helped her out . . .

I HOPE YOU BOYS WERE LISTENING TO MY TALK ABOUT DEODORANT!

YEAH . . . CUZ MOST OF YOU SMELL LIKE #@$✗!

HAN ROLO + FORTUNE COOKIEE *

HAN ROLO AND THE FORTUNE COOKIEE

BY SARA

So, the first hour of my trip was this:

Rhondella: [Looking at phone.] He hasn't written yet!

Rhondella: [Hiding phone.] When is he going to write?

Rhondella: [Looking at phone.] He hasn't written yet!

Rhondella: [Hiding phone.] When is he going to write?

Rhondella: [Looking at phone.] He hasn't written yet!

Rhondella: [Shoving phone in my face.] OMG!!! It's from
    him!!!! OMG! He did send a selfie!!!! OMG!
    Isn't he cute? Look, Sara. Look! ⟶

Rhondella: [Looking at phone.] I gotta send one back to

✳ ARTIST'S RENDERING. IN REALITY, SARA
WAS TALKING TO A CHOCOLATE GLOB AND
A FACELESS BROKEN COOKIE.

him. Make sure Rabbski isn't looking while I take it. I wish my hair wasn't wonked!

[FOURTEEN SECONDS OF BLESSED SILENCE.]

Rhondella: [Shoving phone in my face.] OMG, here's another one. It's. Even. Cuter!

This is what I had been looking forward to? This is what I ditched Tommy for?

If I had Darth Paper, I would have stood up and yelled, "NOOOOOOOO!" Actually, I realized, if I had my Fortune Wookiee, he might have been able to help me out of this mess!

But I had followed Rabbski's rule and left Chewie and Han Foldo at home. And, actually, that had been one of Rhondella's rules, too, when I asked her to sit with me.

"Well," I thought, "at least Rhondella's drippy boyfriend will be at school soon and the texting will stop and then I'll get her to myself for a while."

But then she said, "OMG, SARA! He's going to sneak his phone into school today! So we can text all day long! He's soooooooooo sweeeeeeet!"

I was just about to hide under the seat for the rest of the trip, when everybody on our side of the bus started pointing out the window.

It was one of the fancy buses passing us. It was hard to see through the tinted windows on their bus—ours didn't have tinted windows, of course—but it looked like they were all waving and yelling.

Then I saw somebody who HAD to be AMY (judging by the hair), and next to her was a skinny shadow (Lance!) waving some sort of blob at me. And then behind him was someone tall—Harvey?—definitely waving some sort of black thing at me. And leaning over in front of him was . . . Tommy! It must have been. Or maybe that was just who I wanted to see.

Anyway, I think it was.

And then, suddenly, smooshed up against the glass was a blob . . . with BIG EARS! . . . YODA! Dwight had made an Origami Yoda somehow! But then it looked like he ate it . . .

And then I realized Tommy was waving a puppet, too. It looked sort of like . . . Big Bird? **✳**

"I wish I was with you," I mouthed at him.

✳ NOBODY CAN FIGURE OUT WHAT SARA IS TALKING ABOUT.

All that happened in about ten seconds as the fancy bus cruised by us and headed on down the highway, leaving us in the dust . . .

BUT I was better off than I had been. I realized what you guys had done. You made *Star Wars* characters out of your snacks! (Well, Yoda was the only one I really recognized, but I mean, duh, what else are you guys going to make?) I hoped Rabbski hadn't looked closely enough to see them!

And now I knew how to get the help I needed.

Rhondella was still YIPPY-YAPPY and peeking at her phone every two seconds, then hiding it again, then getting it out again . . . infinity.

I got out my snack bag.

The FORCE was with me! Gingersnaps . . . not only my favorite cookie . . . but only a couple of snaps away from being a fairly decent Fortune Wookiee . . . make that a Fortune Cookiee!

(Kellen, please draw a picture for me!)

Well, of course, it didn't work like the real Fortune Wookiee, with flaps to lift to get answers, but I was sure it would help. I spelled out "Help me, Chewbacca, you're my only hope" and landed in the lower-left portion of the cookie. I turned it over and . . . Of course there weren't words on the cookie. But the message was in my head: "RGGGHHRRRRWWWRR!!!"

Oh, no! I needed Han Foldo to translate!

I had a couple of granola bars. I guess one would sort of look like Han in carbonite, but what good would that do me? He couldn't talk while in the carbonite.

"Rhondella, can I see your snacks?" I asked.

She handed her bag over without looking up from her phone.

"Maybe she's got some ham for Ham Solo," I thought. "Or flan! Her family is always eating flan! Flan Solo to the rescue! . . . But, no . . . just an entire bag of Hershey's Kisses."

"I'd sooner kiss a Wookiee!" I thought . . . But that didn't do me any good, either.

So I started asking around . . . and struck gold! Cassie had brought Rolos! HAN ROLO!

I used my fingernail to scratch a smiley on one. It didn't look much like Han Solo (picture, please, Kellen!) . . .

I'M A DELICIOUS MIX OF CHOCOLATE + CARAMEL, KID!

. . . BUT IT WORKED!

"Chewie says the phone's got to go!"

"But how?" (This was all in my head, by the way.)

Chewie: GRRRRR!

Han: He says, "Throw it out the window, kid!"

Me: No way! Rhondella would make me pay for it!
Rabbski would kick me out of school!

Han: Oh, yeah, Rabbski . . . She's tougher than
Bossk on a bad day! She'll handle it for you . . .

Me: How can . . .

Han: You need to think like a scoundrel, kid!

I was better at thinking like a scoundrel than I
expected. I figured it out in about thirty seconds. The
answer was so simple!

I snuck across the aisle to whisper with Jen. I knew
she had smuggled a phone on board the bus, too!

"I've got a Ventress-style job for you," I whispered.
"Wait ten minutes. Then call Rhondella. Hang up and
hide your phone before she answers."

"Can't I just text her?"

HUH? HOW IS THIS A "VENTRESS-STYLE JOB?"

I'M A RENEGADE SITH TURNED BOUNTY HUNTER, NOT A TELEPHONE OPERATOR!

"No, you need to call."

"But—"

"Shhh! If she ever asks why you called, keep my name out of it. Just say you must have butt-dialed her by accident . . ."

"But—"

"I'll explain later. And . . . I'll owe you one."

I don't think Rhondella even noticed I had talked to Jen. She was busy taking more photos of herself to send to that dumb boyfriend.

"Let me take one," I said. "I'll get a better angle."

"Okay, but be careful not to let Rabbski see my phone," she whispered.

I took a photo and may have "accidentally" turned the ringer on. Then I gave her the phone and she went back to her boyfriend.

And then about ten minutes later, her phone rang! It went off SUPER LOUD!!! Her ringtone was blaring: "UH-HUH! KISS THIS KISS!!! UH-HUH! KISS ME! KISS THIS—"

Then it suddenly stopped before Rhondella could even switch it off.

Rabbski was on top of us before the echo had died away . . .

The phone was confiscated. Rhondella grumbled for half an hour.

And then I had her to myself the rest of the day!

Harvey's Comment

A brilliant plan, Sara! MoST IMPRESSIVE!

My Comment: Wow, I have to agree. I didn't know Sara was capable of scoundrel-like behavior!

PICKLETINE VS. APPLESEED

BY MIKE

I'm getting a little annoyed with my job as Holocron Keeper.

It was one thing when we were battling the forces of Edu-Fun Evil . . . but now I'm basically just cataloging Harvey's complaints, whines, and rudities. (That's a Murky-ism . . . It means "rude statements.")

And as annoying as Harvey is on his own, he's even more annoying when he's wiggling his Emperor Pickletine at you and making him insult you:

EDU FUN EVIL! THAT'S ME!

"I find that you are mistaken . . . about a great many things."

"Can you chew more quietly, puny human?"

"It is as I have foresmelled . . . Those pitiful bagel chips have made your breath smell like feet."

"Yes . . . Good . . . I can feel your anger! Soon your journey to the Sour Side will be complete."

It's probably for the best that Rabbski confiscated the Holocron, so I didn't feel obligated to write it all down. Those are just the ones I remember.

Of course, I remember the whole Johnny Appleseed Incident perfectly!

Amy goes, "Oh, look, a giant statue of Johnny Appleseed."

Nobody looks.

"No, seriously, guys—look!"

Nobody looks.

"LanLan . . . I order you to look! Quick!!!!"

(LanLan is her disturbing boyfriend name for Lance.)

No! You MAY NOT DRAW MY BUTT EITHER!

Lance looks.

"Holy Wampa Heinie! It IS a giant Johnny Appleseed!"

At this point, all the other kids on the bus were looking out that side, too, and saying, "Johnny Appleseed!"—or in one case, "Justin Bieber holding an apple!"

So I figured it was safe to look. And so did Quavondo, Tommy, and Dwight.

IT WAS STOOKY!!!!!!! There really, really, actually was a huge statue of Johnny Appleseed in front of a restaurant!

But Harvey WOULD NOT LOOK! And by that time, we had passed it.

"Another pitiful attempt . . . and another point for me, the true champion of this game!"

"But it was real, Harvey."

"Uh-huh. I'm sure it was. Now I get a point for everybody that claimed they saw it . . . about six, I should say. Making me the winner and true cham—"

"No, you idiot," said Amy. "It WAS there. You

get nothing! You should get negative points for missing it!"

"Wrong!" spat Emperor Pickletine. "You'll never trick me, foolish girl!"

"I am not wrong! You are wrong! And a butt! And if you ever talk to me like that again—" At this point Amy was leaning across the aisle and trying to squash Pickletine!

"Okay, fine," said Harvey. "Believe any little thing your little brain wants to! I'm wrong, and there really is a giant Johnny Appleseed. And he has a magic apple that sings songs and . . ."

"HE WAS THERE, HARVEY!" yelled Tommy. "WE ALL SAW HIM!"

"Of course you did, Tommy Toes," said Harvey. "YOU—"

"Is there a problem back here?" said Miss Bauer. "Where is your chaperone? Mr. Good Cl— Er . . . Adam?"

Mr. Good Clean Fun stuck his head out of the tiny bathroom.

NOOOO...NOT...SPRINKLING!

"Just giving the potty a little midtrip cleaning!" he said, slathering his hands with sanitizer. Then he whispered: "There's been some sprinkling . . ."

"Well," said Miss Bauer. "There's been some yelling out here and I think—"

"I've got just the thing for that," said Mr. Good Clean Fun. "Another SING-ALONG! We'll turn these GRUMPERS into GRINNERS!"

So he taught us this song called "Anger Is the Most Contagious Germ," and we all had to sing the chorus with Soapy and pretend we were washing our hands.

Out! out! O#! Spot!

"Scrub. Scrub. Scrub out the anger!"

Miss Bauer stomped back to her seat. It definitely did not look like she had scrubbed all her anger out!

But the song actually worked, sort of. It did settle everything down as far as no more yelling, but Amy looked like she was about to explode and we had to cancel the "Made You Look" game for the rest of the trip.

LOOK, SIR, DROIDS!

SHUTTUPP!

Cancel the game? Oh, no . . . I'm afraid it wasn't canceled. It was WON . . . by me! You all just gave up because I AM THE SUPREME MASTER OF THE GAME FOR ALL TIME!!!!!!!!!! BOW BEFORE ME, INSIGNIFICANT HUMANS!!!!!

My Comment: Excuse me, Supreme Master? Maybe you'd like to take a look at this picture, which Jen took with her smuggled cell phone when her bus went past the statue . . .

Harvey's Second Comment

No comment.

84

TOP 5 WEIRD THINGS DWIGHT DID ON THE BUS

BY KELLEN

1) Dwight put his seat back while going, "Pshhhhh." Then he let it come forward with a "Cha-kawwwww-pfft." Put his seat back while going, "Pshhhhh." Let it come forward with a "Cha-kawwwww-pfft." Put his seat back while going, "Pshhhhh." Let it come forward with a "Cha-kawwwww-pfft." REPEAT, until Mr. Good Clean Fun told him to stop. I think it was seriously the only time Mr. GCF told any of us to stop doing anything the whole trip.

I'M ABOUT TO #@!=$ LOSE MY @!X!$ MIND!

CHAKAWWWPFFT
CHAKAWWWPFFT
CHAKAWWPFFT

YEP! I JT IT LOST IT!

CLILKCLIKCLIKCLIKCLIK
LKCILKCLIKCLIKCLIK
CLIKCILKCLIKCLIKCLIK
CLIKCLIKCLIKCLIKCLIK
CLICKCILIA CIIL

2) After that, he just clicked the button for putting the seat back about . . . oh, I'd guess: 2 million times.

3) Every time we hit a bump—and there were a lot of them—Dwight would go "WAH!" and throw whatever he was holding up in the air, like the bump was fifty times bigger than it was. EVERY TIME!!!!

WAH!

4) He went to the bathroom. And then when he tried to come out, he kept rattling the door. Then we heard him yelling, "Squirrels, come save me!!!" So I yelled, "Dwight, there's a little latch you have to flip." A second later he comes out like absolutely nothing had happened. Of course, he forgot to use a paper towel on the door latch. So Mr. GCF made him go back in to wash again. Next thing I know he's shouting, "Squirrels, come save me!" AGAIN! "Dwight! Flip the latch WITH A PAPER TOWEL!!!!" I yelled.

SORRY. NO WAY I WAS GOING ANYWHERE NEAR THAT STINKHOLE BATHROOM.

I LIKE NUTS.

5) Since his snack was all Fruit Roll-Ups, I gave Dwight some Cheetos. A small handful, maybe six or seven. By the time he was done with the Cheetos, his entire shirt was covered in orange fingerprints! How is it even scientifically possible? It was only six Cheetos! They don't have THAT much orange powder on them!

Harvey's Comment

Kellen, you have my sympathy. You got the worst bus buddy, but you handled it with grace and dignity.

My Comment: The worst bus buddy? Er, I didn't know it was a contest, but I CAN think of another possible winner! <cough> Harvey <cough>ingham <cough>.

Kellen's Comment

YEAH, ACTUALLY, I'M NOT COMPLAINING ABOUT DWIGHT —WELL, MAYBE NUMBER TWO. HE WAS A PRETTY FUN BUS BUDDY. AND AT LEAST HE DIDN'T [REMOVED FOR SPOILER ALERT REASONS] LIKE HARVEY DID!

NEWS FROM
THE SLOW BUS

BY CASSIE

Tommy, Cassie here.

Jen loaned me her phone so I could e-mail you a live report from our bus. I know you won't get it until you get home, but there's not much else to do right now, so:

The good news: Sherlock Dwight was right, we did stop at a rest stop! So much better than peeing on the bus!!

The bad news: Riding with Rabbski AND Howell isn't exactly Happy Happy Fun Fun! Rabbski settled down after a jittery start, but nobody wants to start her off again by acting too crazy or making too much noise. ☹

As for Howell's buddy bunch . . . they're afraid to

RABBSKI   HOWELL

move! He's griped at them about every little thing, so now they are just sitting quietly. Poor little things! ☹

Well, Jen wants her phone back because she's afraid Rabbski is going to catch me, so . . .

P.S. Sara says: xoxoxoxo

P.P.S. Say hi to Kellen for me.

Harvey's Comment

If I had realized how much the toilet on the bus was going to smell, I would have listened to Sherlock Dwight, too. Can no one figure out how to get the smell to blow out the back of the bus instead of forward into the seating area? This awful mix of normal bathroom smells and highly toxic brain-eating chemicals that are supposed to smell like flowers. I think it ate away at my brain cells . . . it's like funtime in a bottle.

My Comment: The bathroom smelled bad? Gee I didn't notice . . . BECAUSE SOMEONE WAS WAVING A PICKLE IN MY FACE FOR HALF THE TRIP!!!!!!!!

Also . . . What's with Cassie's P.P.S.? Could she be . . .? Does this mean . . . ? Is she . . . ?

THE REST OF THE BUS TRIP

BY TOMMY

After that, things were a little unpleasant and a lot boring.

Amy was genuinely mad and spent all her time grumbling to Lance.

Harvey kept right on complaining and making Pickletine chuckle and be nasty.

I spent all my time wishing I had picked a different seat partner. I begged Kellen to switch with me, but he was like: "Are you crazy?"

Plus, he and Dwight were busy trying to fold a Van Jahnke Yoda from a fruit roll-up.

BEST.
T.V.
DOG.
EVER. →
K9

Quavondo and Mike were trying to think of every famous dog from TV, books, and movies, but because of where they were sitting it was hard for me to keep up with them, and every time I suggested something—Rowlf of the Muppets, for example—they would say, "Already got him." So that got boring, too.

The one interesting thing that happened before we got to D.C. was when we turned off Interstate 81 onto Interstate 66.

"Execute Order 66," the bus driver said over his microphone. We had the coolest bus driver in the world! Unlike a lot of adults, this dude knew his prequel plot points!

I thought turning onto a different road meant we were getting close, but we just kept going and going.

Finally, we started seeing stuff. First, the road got really wide, with lots of narrow lanes. Then tons of traffic. Then the subway—which is aboveground in some places. Then we were crossing a bridge and we saw the Washington Monument!

ORDER 66?
THAT'S A BIG
10-4 GOOD
BUDDY!

JEFF

ABE

KIT

Miss Bauer got on the microphone and started telling us what to look at:

The Jefferson Memorial. The Lincoln Memorial. The Kit Fisto Memorial. Etc., etc.

We stopped at the Washington Monument, and we all got out and walked around and touched it, but we didn't get to go up in it. Miss Bauer told us about how one of the stones in it was from near where we live.

Then we walked to the Lincoln Memorial and back.

MAY THE FORCE BE WITH YOU!!

Then we drove past the White House, which was pretty cool, but we didn't get out. And then we drove past the Capitol and stopped

MALL?

at the National Mall, which isn't really a mall. It's just the empty space between all the museums. And the bus dropped us off near where the other buses from school were. I couldn't wait to see Sara, but her bus wasn't there yet.

Our bus driver unloaded the coolers so we could get out our lunch bags, and then he

YAY! THIS BUTTWICH IS STILL FRESH!

drove away to park the bus somewhere. Lance asked him what he was going to do while we went into the museum.

"Clean up the crud you kids have dropped all over my bus," he said. Maybe he wasn't so cool after all.

So then we went with Mr. Good Clean Fun to look for a place to eat lunch.

All the other buddy bunches got to sit under trees. But Mr. Good Clean Fun said that was a perfect place to get a "topping of bird dropping" on your sandwich. So we had to stand around on the sidewalk.

Harvey's Comment

I lost my appetite after he said "topping of bird dropping."

My Comment: Yeah, and then he made us all use another round of hand sanitizer. It left my hands so smelly, I could barely eat my sandwich without gagging.

I kept waiting for Sara's bus to get there! But it was

MMM . . .
JUST WHAT THIS
BUTTWICH NEEDED!

so slow!!!! It was starting to seem like I wouldn't even see Sara all day because her buddy group was going to a different museum.

Seeing some of the buildings had been kind of cool, but so far this field trip wasn't the sort of life-changing adventure that Origami Yoda had predicted! We had fought so hard for it . . . and now it was starting to seem like it wasn't worth it.

But then things got ~~better~~ . . .

WORSE!

NOSTRUL! PIK POK! GRUNDLY! TOTAL FISHMASTER DISASTER! I'VE GOT A BAD FEELING ABOUT THIS! BLU-RAY NOOOOOOO!

SPUGLY!

PANTS

BEFORE

ORIGAMI YODA AND THE EMBARRASSING STAIN, EPISODE II

BY KELLEN

Why me?

How come I'm the one who always ends up looking like an idiot THROUGH NO FAULT OF MY OWN?

Whose fault was it this time? Lance's! My EX-FRIEND Lance! ──────────→

You remember the rule about packing your lunch on this trip, right? We were supposed to bring a bottle of water or maybe juice or something like that. NO SODA was the rule! NO SODA!!!!

I AM DUM

BANTHA DUNG →

It turns out there was a very good reason for that, beyond just the high-fructose corn syrup and stuff.

So, we're all standing around because Mr. Good Clean Fun wouldn't let us sit down to eat. Everybody is unpacking their lunches and wishing they had brought something better. (Everyone except Dwight, who was perfectly happy because he had brought a frozen Rib-B-Q patty that had only thawed partway, so it was basically a Rib-B-Q-Sicle.)

Lance: Look at this, dudes! I have in my hands the stookiest thing ever!

[Well, that seemed worthy of hitting the REC button for.]

Harvey: The same nasty, stained water bottle you bring to school every day? Whoopie!

[For once, I was in complete agreement with Harvey.]

Lance: That's the beauty of it! It looks

the same as always. But it's not the same as always. I figured out how to do this field trip in style!

Me (Kellen): With a stained water bottle?

Lance: Dude, it's what's IN the water bottle that counts.

Harvey: Okay, could we just skip to the end of this? What is in the water bottle?

Lance: Mountain Dew!

Mike: You're not allowed to have soda for lunch!

Lance: Duh, I know! That's why it's hidden in my usual water bottle.

Before I go any further, I need to tell you what Lance's water bottle was like, in case you're somebody reading this case file one hundred years from now and don't know what I'm talking about.

It's a plastic bottle that once upon a time had Yoda and a couple of clone troopers on

DUDE! YOU'RE NOT LOOKING SO GOOD.

I'VE LEARNED A VALUABLE LESSON.

it. They are mostly rubbed off or covered in grime by now. On top is a screw-on lid with this really grungy straw that sticks out. The straw has its own screw-on cap so that water doesn't leak out.

"So, you guys enjoy your water while I take a big swig of DEW!" said Lance.

"Wait, wait . . . ," said Dwight.

And Dwight started folding up a Fruit Roll-Up.

But Lance didn't wait. He was reaching for the straw cap.

The Fruit Roll-Up was starting to look like Yoda. Just another two folds to go . . .

Lance's fingers started to unscrew the straw cap . . .

The Fruit Roll-Up now looked like Origami Yoda and Dwight shoved it on his finger.

"Carbonation . . . a powerful ally it is . . . ," said Origami Yoda, "but beware of—"

The cap came off.

The Mountain Dew exploded out of the straw!

A bright yellow streak arced through the air, right across the sidewalk . . .

. . . shimmering for a moment in the bright sunlight . . .

. . . dancing in the air, with the Washington Monument and the cherry trees as a backdrop . . .

. . . like a yellow rainbow over our nation's capital . . .

. . . a yellow rainbow that ended . . . on my pants!

And you know WHERE on my pants it landed, right?

AFTER

Harvey and Tommy went into hysterics. Amy was like, "Oh, My Nox!!" And Lance just stood there with a big, dumb Jar Jar smile!

And then suddenly, another whole busload of kids was unloading right there onto the sidewalk!

"NOOO!" I thought. "Not . . ."

But it was . . . It was Rhondella's bus.

And there she was . . .

She didn't laugh. Everybody else from that whole bus laughed, but she didn't.

And somehow that made it even worse.

"It's not pee! It only LOOKS LIKE PEE!" yelled Lance as they all trooped past. And that DEFINITELY made it worse.

So I'm standing there on the National Mall with a big stain that looks like pee but isn't pee and I know finally, once and forever, that I will never, ever, ever have a chance with Rhondella. The dream is dead.

Fruitigami Yoda: All of pants you must wet.

Me: Great . . . thanks . . .

Harvey's Comment

→ **Dew or Dew not, there is no dry!**

My Comment: Oh, man, that WAS hysterical . . . but I am sorry about the timing with Rhondella and everything, Kellen. But trust me, it wasn't the Mountain Dew's fault. Rhondella just doesn't like you.

TURTLE!!!!

BY LISA

Tommy, do your case files absolutely have to be about *Star Wars* and origami? Because this one doesn't have either, but our part of the field trip was so awful that we feel like it needs to be remembered in some way. I'm thinking about cross-stitching it on a pillow for Mrs. Porterfield, but since I don't know how to cross-stitch, that may not happen.

Me and Jacob both signed up to be in Mrs. Porterfield's group so we could go to the Natural History Museum with her.

She was very excited for us to see the glyptodon. That's

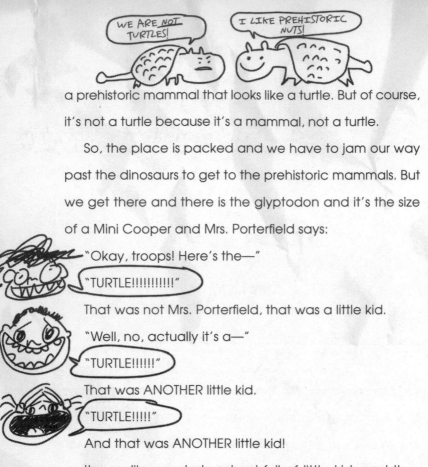

a prehistoric mammal that looks like a turtle. But of course, it's not a turtle because it's a mammal, not a turtle.

So, the place is packed and we have to jam our way past the dinosaurs to get to the prehistoric mammals. But we get there and there is the glyptodon and it's the size of a Mini Cooper and Mrs. Porterfield says:

"Okay, troops! Here's the—"

"TURTLE!!!!!!!!!!!!"

That was not Mrs. Porterfield, that was a little kid.

"Well, no, actually it's a—"

"TURTLE!!!!!!"

That was ANOTHER little kid.

"TURTLE!!!!!"

And that was ANOTHER little kid!

It was, like, a whole school full of little kids and they were all tied to each other and every single one had to yell "TURTLE!!!!!"

And Mrs. Porterfield kept trying to tell them what it really was and they were drowning her out: "TURTLE TURTLE TURTLE TURTLE TURTLE."

"Would you like me to explain what this really is?" Mrs. Porterfield asked the teacher of the little kids. And that teacher gave her a look like, "Whatever."

So Mrs. Porterfield goes, "Now, I know this looks a lot like a turtle, but it's really a—"

"TURTLE!!!!"

This was ANOTHER whole group of kids that were coming in from the dinosaur hall.

"TURTLE! TURTLE! TURTLE!!!!!"

Now it was so crowded that we were all basically pushed on into the next room, where there was a mammoth.

"Well!" said Mrs. Porterfield. "I guess we may as well look at this—"

"ELEPHANT! ELEPHANT!!! ELEPHANT!!!!!!!"

Harvey's Comment

The glyptodon is my favorite prehistoric mammal. A lot of people don't realize its importance in the early ice-age ecosystem. There are actually four major types of [The rest of this comment has been deleted.]

My Comment: TURTLE!

PAPER AIRPLANES

BY LANCE

Okay, I'll write this chapter, since I was the one that started the whole thing.

After the Mountain Dew incident, we went into the Air and Space Museum.

It was nice . . . walking around looking at space stuff while holding hands with Amy and making dumb jokes to try to cheer up Kellen.

We had all come out of that exhibit about rockets. Which, by the way, was "total rockets!"

Then Dwight had to go to the bathroom, so we were all waiting around for him.

We were in that giant, giant room that takes up most of the museum and is, like, five stories tall and has all those amazing airplanes and spaceships and things hanging down from the ceiling. And since we were on the second floor, we were standing at the railing of the balcony part looking out at all the stooky stuff. Even if they don't have the *Millennium Falcon*, you still can't help but look at all those planes and rockets and space capsules and stuff and say, "Wow!"

"You know," I said, "this would be the most massively waffle-tastic place in the universe to throw a paper airplane!"

"Great idea, Lance!" said Kellen, waving his Treasure Hunt worksheet. "Let's DO IT!"

Oh, if you weren't on the field trip, you won't know what worksheet I'm talking about. Miss Bauer handed out these worksheets to us when we split up to go see the museums. It was the only piece of paper we were allowed to have all day!

It had a big grid inside a treasure chest and you had to fill out boxes that said stuff like: "The biggest thing you saw." "The most valuable thing you saw."

HARVEY'S
NOSE

We know you'll DIG D.C.!!!!

Fill in the chart below with the _____ thing you saw.
Ex. The BEST thing!!!!!

BEST!	OLDEST	MOST IMPORTANT	MOST VALUABLE	WEIRDEST
IMPORTANT TO US HISTORY	IMPORTANT TO WORLD HISTORY	FIRST	LAST	WORST? (IF ANY)
CONFUSING (Want to learn more about it?)	MOST BEAUTIFUL	FREE PARKING	FASTEST	SLOWEST
ENERGY-EFFICIENT	ECO-FRIENDLY	BIGGEST	smallest	FAMOUS
TALLEST	BREATH-TAKING	MOST RADICOOL	FAVORITE	INSPIRING

"The oldest thing you saw." And on and on. There were, like, twenty-five boxes. I had only filled in three so far.

So, like I was saying, Kellen held his worksheet up and said, "Let's do it."

And Amy goes: "Do you know how much trouble you'll get in for that?"

LALALA PAPER CUT!

"With Mr. Good Clean Fun?" I said. "Who cares? He'll just make us sing a song about paper cuts or something."

"What about the people who get hit on the head with your airplane, smart-butt?" said Amy.

LALALA PAPER CUT!

"Okay, they can sing, too."

"NO, I mean what about when they get mad at you?"

"No problem," said Kellen. "We watch the planes glide a ways, then we all go to the bathroom, too. By the time they hit the ground, there will be nothing but an empty balcony to look at up here."

"I still think we could get into trouble," said Mike.

"Fine, don't do it," said Kellen. "But so far this field trip has been totally nostrul and I am going to do at least one completely stooky thing today that's worth remembering."

FROM TINY PAPER CUTS, BIG INFECTIONS SPREAD!

THAT'S HOW BIB FORTUNA GOT THOSE THINGS ON HIS HEAD!

"I think we should ask Origami Yoda first," said Mike.

Harvey pulled Pickletine out of his shirt pocket just enough for his pickley face to stick out.

"Oh . . . I'm afraid you'll find that your pitiful Jedi friend is still in the bathroom with Dwight."

I was about to tell Harvey to shut it, when Kellen said: "Perfect! Thank you, Harvey."

And Harvey was all, "Whuh?"

Kellen went over to Mr. Good Clean Fun. "You might want to check on Dwight. He's not back from the bathroom yet."

Mr. GCF—who had been wiping the balcony railing with a moist towelette—went off to the bathrooms.

"If Kit Fisto was here, he'd be very disappointed by your lies and treachery!" said Quavondo.

"Who's lying?" asked Kellen. "Dwight ISN'T back from the bathroom and he probably DOES need someone to go look for him."

"Well," said Quavondo, "then, I'm going, too, because you guys are going to get in huge trouble." And he went off after Mr. GCF.

"Okay," I said, "how fast can you guys fold?"

I'M VERY DISAPPOINTED BY KELLEN'S LIES AND— OH, WAIT? PAPER AIRPLANES? HECK YES!

INVENTED BY EIJI NAKAMURA!

THE LOCK PART

"I wish I had my *Star Wars* Flyers book!" said Tommy. "It's got some amazing airplanes in it!"

"Dude," I said, "there's no time. Fold a Nakamura Lock and get ready to throw."

In case you don't know, the Nakamura Lock is one of the best airplanes ever invented—it flies great AND it is pretty quick and easy to fold. I have a modified version I like to use that only has ten folds.

"Want me to make you one, Amy?" I asked when I saw she wasn't folding.

"I'm perfectly capable of making my own plane," she said, "but in this case I'll remain a spectator."

"I'm folding my Flying Vader," said Harvey.

"Uh, Vader doesn't fly," said Kellen.

FLYING VADER

"This one does," said Harvey. "Now be quiet so I can concentrate."

Harvey, who had been talking nonstop Dark Side narnar all day, asks US to be quiet! HA!

"I wish I had some tape," said Tommy, which—I'm sorry, dude—is a very embarrassing thing to say.

A TAPE OF THE CLONES!

"Okay, everybody ready?" I asked, holding up my NakLock (pronounced "Nock Lock").

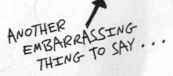

ANOTHER EMBARRASSING THING TO SAY . . .

"Yep," said Kellen.

"Just a minute," said Harvey.

"We don't have a minute!" I said.

"Well, I'm not finished yet!"

"Too bad, dude. Let's throw all together, in five . . ."

". . . and get ready to run for the bathroom!" said Kellen.

"Four . . ."

"I'm not done!" said Harvey.

"Three . . ."

"I'm going to regret this," said Mike.

"Hey, that's MY line," I said. "Two . . ."

"I'm not doing it," said Mike.

"Let me tweak the elevator flaps and adjust the dihedrals!" whined Harvey.

"One . . ."

"All right, I'm doing it," said Mike.

Amy kissed me on the cheek.

"For luck," she said. "And now I'm getting out of here because I have a bad feeling about this."

Me, personally, I had a great feeling about it. I could tell I had a great plane. I tapped the wings up just a bit for lift and . . .

KELLEN'S
TOMMY'S
LANCE'S

"THROW!" I whispered loudly.

We all threw—me, Kellen, and Tommy. (Mike chickened out and didn't throw his.)

Tommy's—which was just a basic glider with some fins—actually flew fairly well, doing a decent stair-step pattern and going fairly straight toward the windows on the far side of the museum.

The Nakamura Locks folded by me and Kellen were amazing! Mine started to do a loop, went way up, stalled out, and then started the most amazing float you have EVER seen!

Kellen hadn't gone for extra lift, so his started a long, fast arc all the way across the space, just curving left a tiny bit.

Then Harvey goes: "ARGGH! I told you to wait!"

ARGHH!

Then he flings his Flying Vader over the edge.

And I forgot all about watching mine fly. (In fact, I never found out where it landed!)

All I could do was watch Flying Vader.

HARVEY'S

Just like I said . . . Vader doesn't fly . . .

It fell like it had been blasted out of the sky by the *Millennium Falcon*. I seriously didn't know paper could fall that fast.

OH POOP!

111

I forgot about running for the bathroom . . . I stood there like an idiot and looked over the railing to watch it crash and . . .

well . . .

it did crash . . .

onto . . .

onto . . .

No. I can't say it. It's too horrible. It's too terrible.

"We're doomed," I whispered as I looked over the railing at . . .

at . . .

at . . .

at Mr. Howell.

Flying Vader had dropped like a rock just as Mr. Howell was walking out from underneath the balcony we were on.

It hit him on the head.

He looked at it.

Then he looked up at us.

Then there was a disturbance in the Force.

THE FLYING VADER WOULD HAVE OUT-FLOWN ALL OF YOURS IF YOU HAD GIVEN ME ONE MINUTE TO ADJUST THE DIHEDRALS!!!!

My Comment: What Lance saw is different from what I saw, because I didn't see Harvey throw the FALLing Vader. I was too busy watching Kellen's plane . . .

EVER NOTICE HOW MR. HOWELL LOOKS LIKE THE GIANT SPACE SLUG FROM THE ASTEROID CAVE? IN A MINUTE HE'S GOING TO BE WORSE! WUG!

SOUND BARRIER

BELL X-1

THE BELL X-1

BY TOMMY

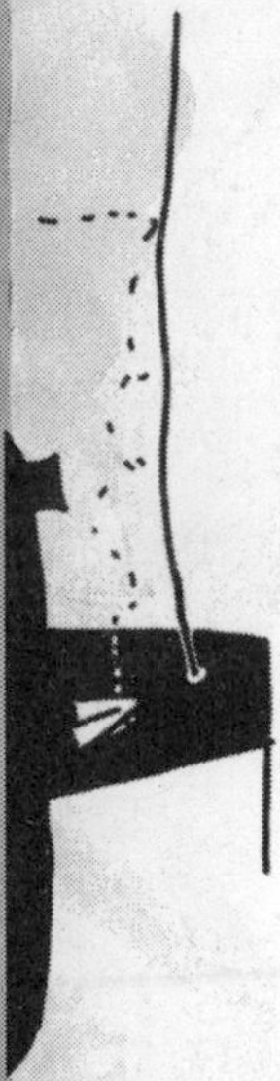

So, I was watching my plane go and Kellen's was up above it—admittedly flying better than mine—and then all of a sudden: BLAP! Kellen's plane hit one of the cables that they use to hang the planes from the ceiling. And Kellen's plane just went THWACK and then dropped down . . . ONTO THE WING OF THE ACTUAL PLANE! Then it just sat there.

"Wug . . . ," Kellen and I croaked at the same time.

Then we heard a voice! A loud voice. A

Voice from Below that filled the entire museum
. . . with fear.

"YOU!!!!!!!!!!!"

I looked down to see Mr. Howell rubbing his
head and bellowing up at us.

Then there was another voice.

"YOU!!!!!!!!!!" This wasn't the Voice from
Below, it was the Voice from Right Behind Us!

We whirled around to see someone else
shouting at us. Someone we had never seen
before. Someone wearing . . . a museum ID
badge.

"DON'T YOU DARE MOVE!!!!!!" This one was
Howell again. We looked back down to see him
quick-marching his buddy bunch toward the up
escalator.

HE WAS COMING FOR US!

"DO you realize what you've DONE?!?!?"
yelled Museum Guy.

He was coming for us, too! And he was a lot
closer. In fact, he was right in our faces!

"Do you realize how much trouble it will

cause to get your airplane off of the Bell X-1?"

"Uh," I said.

"Do you have no respect?! No respect AT ALL? That is the Bell X-1! THE. BELL. X. ONE!"

"Uh," I said.

"Oh, good Lord!" And he threw his hands up in the air. "Where's your chaperone?"

"Uh," I said.

Mr. Good Clean Fun still hadn't come back. Not that he could have protected us.

Mr. Howell came running up.

"Are you their chaperone?" said Museum Guy.

"I AM NOW," bellowed Mr. Howell, glaring at us.

"These children have defiled a national treasure!" said Museum Guy. "Perhaps from your vantage point you didn't notice that one of the planes is now resting on the Bell X-1!"

"NOT THE BELL X-1!" screeched Howell.

"Yes . . . the BELL X-1!!"

"Well," said Lance, "at least it wasn't the Bell X-2 . . ."

"BLURGA WURGA KREEEEEE!" That was the ACTUAL sound Howell made! And I don't think he was doing a Jabba impression, either. That was just what naturally came out of him when he was this angry, which was a record level of angry even for Mr. Howell.

CEN-
SOR-
ED!

TOO
DISTURBING
TO
DRAW

Museum Guy looked at Mr. Howell. Mr. Howell looked at Museum Guy. They were looking at each other with respect, the way you would expect a couple of Hutts to do if they met wherever it is Hutts meet each other.

And then they turned and looked at us the way you would expect a couple of Hutts to look at a couple of frog sandwiches.

"I'm going to need to call in a maintenance crew with a lift to get that paper airplane down," said Museum Guy. And he whipped out a notebook and pen. "And that means I'll need to file an incident report. Names, please."

117

"Hey, everybody," came the cheerful voice of Mr. Good Clean Fun from behind us. "I found Dwight! He was talking to some kid and—Oh, hi, Mr. Howell. Is something wrong?"

I think it was the best moment of Howell's and Museum Guy's lives as they told Mr. Good Clean Fun everything that was wrong and how terrible we were and how much trouble it was going to be to get the plane down, and they did make it sound pretty bad. Mr. Good Clean Fun looked like the tauntaun right before it gets clobbered by the wampa.

And, honestly, I felt like the tauntaun right AFTER it gets clobbered by the wampa.

Dwight, as soon as he walked up, pulled out a .Fruit Roll-Up and started folding. Right around the time that he was finally done and was putting Fruitigami Yoda on his finger, Howell and Museum Guy were loudly explaining to Mr. Good Clean Fun how we had disrespected what was possibly the most important plane in the museum . . . no, the most important item in any museum anywhere on earth.

Museum Guy turned around to point at the plane, with Kellen's bright Nakamura Lock looking like a big white pimple on the wing.

"The Bell X-1! The actual aircraft that, for the first time in human history—"

Fruitigami Yoda interrupted him with an "Urmmmmm." And Dwight held it out over the railing.

"Not now, Dwi—" Mr. Howell was starting.

But then Lance yelled:

"LOOK!"

And Kellen's airplane fell off the Bell X-1. It dropped down into a giant herd of kids from another school and by the time they had walked past, it was just a piece of balled-up paper on the floor.

Was it a sudden gust of wind, even though we were inside?

Or was it . . . the Force?

I turned back to Dwight and he was already eating the Fruit Roll-Up.

"No food in the museum!" snarled Museum Guy.

Dwight swallowed the rest of it whole.

"Well," said Museum Guy, putting away his notebook. "That was very lucky for you, kids. Now there's no need for an incident report. However, I trust that your chaperone will make sure you learn a lesson from this."

"Oh, yes," said Mr. Howell, with a gleam in his eye. "I'll be CERTAIN they do."

And he and Museum Guy gave each other that look again.

"It will be a lesson they NEVER forget," said Howell.

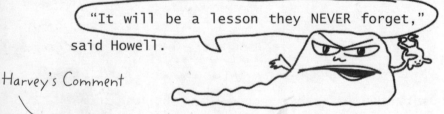

Harvey's Comment

I REPEAT . . . MY PLANE WOULD HAVE FLOWN IF YOU HAD LET ME TWEAK IT!!!!!

My Comment: See, this is why we need Origami Yoda. (Or Fruitigami Yoda.) Everything is going fine. And then Dwight takes Yoda's Jedi wisdom away for ten minutes and everything is a complete disaster.

And then he comes back and saves the day.

Well . . . sort of. Even Origami Yoda is no match for Mr. Howell when he's that mad!

TO LIGHTEN THE MOOD, HERE ARE BOBA + BOSSK RIDING A UNICORN!

SORRY, KELLEN, BUT NO!

WE ARE TOO UPSET BY YOUR BEHAVIOR!

I MEAN, C'MON!! IT WAS THE BELL X-1! SHOW SOME RESPECT!

MR. HOWELL SMILES

BY TOMMY

So, Museum Guy left Mr. Howell to take care of things.

And he did.

First, Howell turned to his own buddy bunch—who had been cowering in fear this whole time—and said, "Mr. Funny Fun will be your chaperone for the rest of the trip. You will be on perfect behavior or I will hear of it. One step out of line and you will be in as much trouble as these creatures"—he waved at us with one claw . . . I mean, hand.

"Take them away, Mr. Funny Fun," he commanded, "and I will take charge of your 'buddy bunch.' I assume you have found all eight of them?"

"Uh, yes . . . well, I think so, uh, two, three, four, uh . . . ," stuttered Mr. Good Clean Fun.

"Good! You may go away now. And . . . Do not fail me again." It sounded EXACTLY like Vader! I'm not sure if that's because Howell was doing a Vader impression or because he is just so in touch with his Dark Side.

"Yes, sir," said Mr. Good Clean Fun very pitifully.

"You're dismissed!" said Mr. Howell.

Then he turned to look at us.

"And now . . . you'll be under my PERSONAL supervision for the rest of the trip," he said. "You'll be riding back on the regular bus with me . . . and Ms. Rabbski. I'm sure she will be delighted to discover that you broke her No Origami rule in such an 'epic' way.

Don't worry . . . I'm sure your punishment will be 'epic,' too!"

And he smiled.

I've never seen a smile like it before. It was a smile of ugly joy.

Harvey's Comment

I can't think of an Anakin or Darth Vader quote that even begins to cover the awfulness of this situation. "Noooooooooo!" has been overused lately. Nor can I think of any quote from any character that comes close. Perhaps if we knew what was going through Boba Fett's mind as he fell into the Sarlacc Pit . . .

My Comment: The Sarlacc Pit feels about right. It digests you alive for a thousand years . . . Our bus ride home was going to feel like a thousand years.

I felt something worse than just the fear of Rabbski yelling at us, though. I felt like . . . well, she had gone to so much trouble to give us our field trip back and now we had ruined it. So now I felt guilty. I mean, I actually felt bad FOR Ms. Rabbski, too. But also terrified OF her.

YEAH...

QUAVONDO'S RESCUE MISSION

BY QUAVONDO

I sure am glad I didn't stick around to see you guys hit Mr. Howell in the head! Well, I kind of wish I had seen it, but I'm very, very, very glad I had a solid alibi and Mr. Good Clean Fun was a witness that I hadn't thrown a plane.

After I left you guys, I went toward the bathroom that Mr. Good Clean Fun had gone to check. When I got there, I heard him hollering from inside, "Excuse me! Is anyone out there? Please open the door for me!"

So I did.

"Thank you, Quavondo," he said. "There were no paper towels in there and I wasn't about to touch the door handle

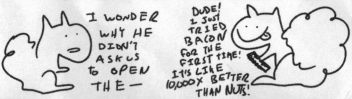

I WONDER WHY HE DIDN'T ASK US TO OPEN THE—

DUDE! I JUST TRIED BACON FOR THE FIRST TIME! IT'S LIKE 10,000× BETTER THAN NUTS!

without a wet wipe, and I left my backpack with the buddy bunch—"

I was afraid he was about to either give a lecture or sing, so I interrupted:

"Was Dwight in there?"

"No, it's empty. Is he the sort that would get lost or wander off?"

"Uh, yeah . . . all of the above," I said.

"We need to find him, A-SAP!" said Mr. Good Clean Fun, looking around the mezzanine. "Unless he went back into the rocket exhibit, he must have gone into one of these two galleries. You check that one, I'll check this one. Do you have a watch? Good. Walk for one minute into the gallery and then for one minute back out, never losing sight of the entrance. I'll do the same. We'll meet back here in two minutes, and if we haven't found him, we'll alert the others."

(I later found out that Mr. Good Clean Fun used to be a paramedic and was trained for this sort of thing!)

But it didn't turn out to be that difficult. Mr. GCF went into a gallery that said FLIGHT AND THE ARTS. I went into one that said TIME AND NAVIGATION.

I found Dwight after about seven seconds. He and another

☐ WANDER OFF
☐ GET LOST
☐ TALK TO STRANGERS
☐ BREAK SOMETHING
☐ MAKE A POTATO MAGICALLY APPEAR
☒ ALL OF THE ABOVE

WILLIAM CRANCH BOND

kid were staring at an exhibit called "Meet the Clock Maker: William Somebody." (Obviously, it didn't say "Somebody." I just can't remember what his name was.)

"Hey, Dwight!" I yelled. "We've got to—"

"It's Captain Dwight," he said. "I've just received a most disturbing report from Captain Micah here."

"Uh . . . Hi, Micah," I said.

"Plesiosaur to meet you," said Micah, continuing to read the plaque about William Somebody.

"Micah has got some big problems at school," Dwight said. "We've been discussing—"

"Dwight!" yelled Mr. GCF, running up behind us.

"Micah!" yelled a lady running toward us from the same direction.

"C'mon, guys, we need to get back to . . ." Mr. Good Clean Fun's words trailed off. He was looking at the lady. She was carrying a can of wet wipes.

"MICAH! Why on earth would you wander off like this? Here, wipe your hands and then we've got to get back to the group." Then she looked at us. "Perhaps you gentlemen would like to sanitize your hands as well?"

I think Mr. GCF was in love at first sight (of the wet

wipes), and if she'd had her own monkey puppet, he would have fallen on his knees and asked her to marry him right on the spot. Instead, he just got her e-mail address—after sanitizing his hands, of course—and then we all went back to find the rest of you guys.

And then you know what happened after that . . .

So I joined you guys in Mr. Howell's chain gang. As he marched us to the bus, we passed the gift shop.

"Aren't we going to the gift shop?" asked Mike.

I thought he was crazy.

"Are you crazy?" snarled Mr. Howell. "You're going straight to the bus to sit quietly while the decent students of this school enjoy the rest of their trip."

"But that's not fair!" said Mike. "I didn't throw a plane and neither did my bus buddy, Quavondo! You're punishing us for something we didn't do!"

"Don't drag me into this," is what I was thinking. And also I was wishing Mace Windu was there to keep Mike cool, because I saw Mike and Mr. Howell face off once last year and it was scary. There had been a lot of Mike's famous "angry tears" and Mr. Howell's famous wampa-like roars.

ACTUALLY, I'D LIKE A CHANCE TO VISIT THE GIFTSHOP, TOO!

But . . . we didn't need Mace after all, because Mr. Howell didn't argue.

"You're right, Mike," he said. "You, Quavondo, Dwight, and Amy are welcome to spend, say, twenty-five minutes in the gift shop. Your comrades will be standing out here with me with their noses touching the wall while hundreds of people walk past laughing at them."

So we went in and looked around. They had a lot of neat stuff. I knew they would. That's why I had brought all my money. I had brought $75 from birthday money and then my grandmother had given me $25 for the field trip, but I knew I needed to spend some of that on something to bring home for my little sister or my grandmother would raise a fuss. (Question: Did my sister bring me home anything from HER field trip? Answer: No.)

I found an awesome-looking kit to make a real rocket out of a plastic soda bottle. And then I got my sister a windup space shuttle I knew she would hate.

Amy was getting Lance a NASA T-shirt. I wish I had a girlfriend like Amy. NOT Amy, but LIKE Amy.

And then Dwight was like, "Quavondo, help me carry these."

And he was basically taking every pack of astronaut ice cream off the rack, but he couldn't even begin to carry them all, especially since he had a new Fruitigami Yoda on his finger.

"Delicious these are!" Fruitigami Yoda said.

"Uh, Dwight . . . ," said Amy. "Don't you think one pack would be plenty?"

"No! Many we must get. Delicious!!!" said Fruitigami Yoda. Unfortunately, when Dwight waved Fruitigami Yoda around to make him talk, he dropped all the packs on the floor.

While we helped him pick them up, I said, "Dwight, I'm not trying to be a Harvey here, but I really don't think you should buy all of these."

"Oh, I'm not buying them," said Dwight. "I'm saving my money for a Wendy's Kids' Meal."

"Then what are we doing with them?" asked Amy.

"We're helping Quavondo buy them," said Dwight.

"WHAT?????????" I said.

Dwight held up Fruitigami Yoda.

"Oh, no!" I said. "Don't say it! Don't make me do it!!!"

"Buy these you must!" said Fruitigami Yoda.

130

"No, please . . . ," I whispered.

"MUST!" Fruitigami Yoda shouted.

"You don't actually have to buy them," said Amy.

"Yes, he does," said Mike. "It is his destiny."

"How much do they cost?" I asked, and then I saw the sign and I almost threw up.

SEVEN DOLLARS! EACH!!!

"Oh, no . . . Please, Yoda . . . That's too much!"

"Wait a second," said Mike. "You can buy a four-pack for twenty dollars. That's only five dollars each."

"ONLY????" said Amy. "Dudes, it's three-quarters of an ounce! You do not want to waste your money on these."

"MUST!" croaked Fruitigami Yoda. Dwight was putting the individual packs back and picking up a bunch of four-packs.

"Woah!" I said. "How many are you getting?"

"Seven," said Dwight.

"Seven???" I gasped. "That will be a hundred and forty dollars! I don't even have that much!"

"How much money DO you have?" asked Mike.

"A hundred dollars . . ."

"You brought a hundred dollars on a field trip?" hissed Amy. "Are you crazy?"

FREEZE DRIED GLOOP $6.99

ASTRO WONDER PACK $20

"I've been saving up! I thought I could get something neat. I didn't know I was going to have to buy this . . . stuff."

"You don't HAVE to, Quavondo. I mean, that's not even Origami Yoda, it's a Fruit Roll-Up."

"Uh, maybe you didn't notice," said Mike, "but Fruitigami Yoda just used the Force to keep your boyfriend from being arrested. He knows what he's talking about. If he says Quavondo needs twenty packs of whatever that stuff is, then Quavondo needs it."

Then Mike got out his wallet and gave me the only thing in it: a twenty.

"I didn't find anything I wanted anyway," he said, which was obviously a total lie because the whole store was stuff Mike wanted.

"Thanks, Mike. But I would still need twenty more dollars."

"Well, I think you're crazy!" said Amy. "But you can borrow—BORROW—this twenty dollars. I had been planning to buy this shirt for Lance, but frankly I'm not in the mood." She tossed the shirt in a bin of astronaut protein sticks.

"Perfect," said Mike. "A hundred and forty dollars! It's like Origami Yoda planned it all out."

"Ugh . . . I guess so," I said.

I put back the rocket kit and my sister's space shuttle and we took the stuff up to the cashier.

I was hoping she would step in and say, "I can't sell you all these, kid."

Instead she rang me up and said, "$148.75."

TAX! I had forgotten about the tax.

"That's all I had," said Mike.

"I can't give you any more," said Amy. "I need to save some for supper."

"What about YOUR supper money, Dwight?" asked Mike.

"Saving it for Wendy's . . ."

"No! Fruitigami Yoda didn't say 'Biggie-size my fries.' He said, 'Must!' Right, Yoda?" Mike asked.

"MUST!" repeated Fruitigami Yoda.

"But—" said Dwight.

"No buts, Dwight! Either you believe in Origami Yoda or you don't. We do weird stuff like this for him all the time and he always has a reason. It's time for YOU to decide. Do YOU believe in him or not?"

Dwight just stared at Fruitigami Yoda.

Fruitigami Yoda stared at Dwight.

133

The cashier was standing there watching all this like we were completely uninteresting in every way. Like puppets made from dried fruit came into the gift shop and talked every day.

"Here," said Dwight. And he gave me his ten dollars. I got a dollar and a quarter back and gave it straight to Dwight, who was looking miserable.

"Maybe you can still get something from the value menu, Dwight," I said. He cheered up immediately.

Then the cashier got out this huge shopping bag and put all the bags of astronaut ice cream in it.

And then I thought with horror of what my parents were going to say when I returned home with a huge sack full of freeze-dried astronaut ice cream and no money! And no supper. And no present for my sister. My grandmother was going to kill me for that last one.

And then I sort of walked out of the store in a daze . . .

Straight into Mr. Howell.

"What on earth have you done now, Quavondo?" Mr. Howell asked. Then he looked in the bag. "HAVE YOU LOST YOUR MIND??????"

"I—" I started.

I TOLD YOU TO GET YOUR SISTER A #!%@PRESENT!

QUAVONDO'S GRANDMOTHER

But he said, "No! No! No more . . . I'm getting all of you on the bus before you do anything else crazy! March! March! GO!"

"You know . . . ," whispered Harvey. "That stuff is so nasty that the astronauts wouldn't actually eat it."

"OH, SHUT UP, HARVEY!" shouted Amy.

And Mr. Howell didn't even fuss at her.

Harvey's Comment

Well, it's true! And what does Quavondo mean by "Being a Harvey"? ←

My Comment: Gee, I don't have any idea . . .

BACK ON THE BUS (WELL, ACTUALLY, ON THE OTHER BUS)

BY AMY

All right, Tommy, you always want a case file . . . well, I'll write one right now while we're waiting on the bus! It's better than talking to any of you—which I am NOT going to be doing!

THAT was embarrassing!

Basically, I rode a bus for five hours with seven sugar-rushing boys so that I could pee in a closet, go into a museum I didn't want to go to, listen to Harvey yak about all the exhibits like he was a tour guide, then get yelled at by Mr. Howell for something I didn't do, then get yelled at again by Mr. Howell for

something I didn't buy, and then get marched halfway across Washington, D.C., with Mr. Howell yelling all the way, and kids from other schools gawking and pointing at us, wondering what we did.

Well, I didn't do ANYTHING except make the terrible mistake of sitting with Lance and the rest of you bantha-brained gundarks! ———————▷

And now, instead of getting to go to the Native American museum like I wanted, I get to sit on the bus for an hour and a half, waiting for everybody else.

Oh, wait, did you think I meant the nice bus we rode here on? . . . Oh, no . . . When Mr. Howell took over our "buddy bunch," he didn't mean he was going to switch to OUR bus, he meant we were going to switch to HIS bus. The cruddy, yellow regular bus.

The kids who started out with Mr. Howell are going to take our seats.

We begged him to let us get our stuff from the other bus. He refused, and not nicely, either.

"But what about me, Mr. Howell?" I asked. "I didn't do anything!"

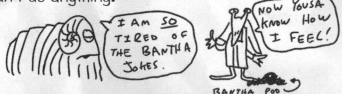

"The last time you told me that, you ran off and helped Quavondo spend $150 bucks on gift shop junk! Now, all eight of you miscreants need to sit here as quietly as possible before I get angry!"

So we sat there and quietly glared at one another. Thankfully, I had kept my notebook with me in my backpack.

There is one upside to switching buses: I'll get to ride with Sara and Cassie and everybody. And it's such a big upside that I actually wonder if the whole thing was one of Origami Yoda's plans. But then I thought it was more like one of the Emperor's schemes, because we were probably going to spend the whole trip getting yelled at by Mr. Howell AND Ms. Rabbski, once she heard the list of broken rules, misdeeds, and disasters.

- - - - - - -

Time passes slowly . . .

- - - - - - -

Okay, finally, here come the other kids . . . and Rabbski . . . and our DOOM.

- - - - - -

WHO, ME?

NO, ME!

Update: Well, that wasn't as bad as I had expected.

Sara and her buddy bunch looked like they had been through heck, too.

For one thing, they had all worn their butt boots, but after all the walking around Washington, D.C., the boots were falling apart and everybody said their feet had blisters.

For another thing, Ms. Rabbski was MAD ... at them, not us!

Mr. Howell tried to tell her what the boys had done with the paper airplanes and Rabbski goes: "Uh-huh ... paper airplanes ... yeah, not even close. I just spent the last HOUR searching the sculpture garden for Jen's lost cell phone—WHICH SHE WAS NOT SUPPOSED TO HAVE ON THE TRIP AT ALL—and at the end of that hour she says, 'Oh ... here it is in my OTHER pocket.'"

"Sorry, Ms. Rabbski!" called Jen, cheerfully. Jen is one of those people who can go through an experience like that and come out of it just as Jen-tastic as ever.

VENUS DE MILO

AS LONG AS YOU'RE LOOKING AROUND, KEEP AN EYE OUT FOR MY ARMS

JEN

SORRY!

If that had been me, I would have felt terrible and felt like I was in huge trouble, and I would have been making the most sincere apologies imaginable. But Jen wasn't the tiniest bit embarrassed, and she actually had a tiny hint of a giggle in her "sorry."

"GRRRRR . . . ," said Ms. Rabbski.

"Well," said Mrs. Porterfield, who had the other buddy bunch on the yellow bus, "at least they weren't as bad as last year's seventh graders . . . We went by the prehistoric mammal exhibit and they still haven't replaced the dire wolf skull that James Suervo Jr. broke last year."

"Oh, Lordy . . . Remind me to yell at him again tomorrow," said Ms. Rabbski.

But they all seemed to have calmed down a bit and only lectured us a little.

And by the time Mr. Howell mentioned Quavondo's giant bag of ice cream, Ms. Rabbski actually laughed. Not a "Hooray, that's fun" laugh. It was more of a "Those crazy kids are on my last nerve" kind of laugh. But still, it WAS a laugh.

The next awful part of all this was when Mr.

Howell's old buddy bunch came on, got their stuff, and left to go take OUR seats on OUR bus. What was that new word for SMUG that Murky invented? That's what they looked like. **MEEFULITO**

When they got off, the bus driver fired up the engine.

I realized that if I was going to switch seats I needed to do it right away.

"Uh . . . Ms. Rabbski? Can we switch bus buddies?"

"Well . . . ," said Ms. Rabbski. "Normally, I would say no, but I'll make an exception in your case because I imagine that those seven boys have driven you up the wall and around the corner. Go ahead."

"Anyone want to switch seats with me?" I called out.

"I will!" said Tommy. "You can have Harvey."

"Anyone else?" I asked.

SILENCE . . .

Nobody wanted to sit with Lance, and who can blame them?

"Why don't YOU go sit with Harvey," I told Lance.

LET'S SING THEM A SONG TO MAKE THE TRIP GO FASTER!

100 NUMERATORS ON THE DENOMINATOR! 100 NUMERATORS! TAKE ONE DOWN, DIVIDE IT AROUND 99 NUMERATORS ON THE DENOMINATOR! 99 NUMERATORS! TAKE ONE DOWN, DIVIDE IT AROUND 98 NUMERATORS ON THE DENOMINATOR! . . .

"Why don't you?"

"I might!" I said. But, of course, I didn't.

I flopped back down on the seat. It was going to be a LONG ride!

"All right, C.J., let's head for home," Rabbski hollered.

"Y'all right," said C.J. And he drove the bus about ten feet before we were stuck in traffic.

"I sure hope the old man got the tractor beam out of commission, or this is going to be a real short trip," said Lance.

"Oh, shut up, Lance," I groaned.

Now I'm going to close this notebook and spend a little time thinking about getting rid of this boyfriend. And, yes, Lance, I know you're reading over my shoulder.

POOR
LAN
LAN!

Lance is fun to hang out with before school and during lunch and maybe at the mall sometimes. But spending a whole day with him and his friends has been sometimes annoying, sometimes embarrassing, and most of the time BOTH!

Harvey's Comment

I have to agree, I was pretty embarrassed by every-one's behavior, too.

My Comment: WHAT???? YOU were the one who—
Oh, forget it!

What a mess! Lance was pretending to be mad, but
I think he was really miserable! I whispered to Kellen to
ask Dwight to ask Fruitigami Yoda for help.

Dwight folded a new Fruit Roll-Up.

It said: "Patience . . . Not over yet is this trip."

Then Dwight ate it.

143

STOOKY MOUNTAIN BREAKDOWN

BY MIKE

I have learned one thing on this field trip: Traffic in Washington, D.C., is insane. I thought Orange Avenue was bad on the way to Roanoke, but this was just crazy.

It took an hour before we got out of the city, and then it was slow for a long time, even though the interstate has, like, twenty lanes or something.

And the fact that everybody on the bus seemed to be furious with someone else on the bus—often their bus buddy—meant no one was having

DUDE...
HE SAID
"MUST!"

fun. Except for some of Mrs. Porterfield's group
. . . they were having like a spontaneous book
club meeting or something.

So we finally get off I-66 and turn onto I-81,
and we see a sign for Roanoke that says: ROANOKE 160
MILES. That's, like, three hours in this slow bus!
And we were all like, "UGH, this trip is going to
take forever." At least we would be stopping for
food soon! I personally was starving.

And then . . .

kachunk kachunk kachunk kachunk

Remember the beginning of *A New Hope*, when
the rebel troopers are waiting for Darth Vader
to bust through the door, and they hear these
weird *kachunk* sounds and look nervously around
at the walls? That.

KACHUNK! And then one really loud one, and
the bus lurched and started shaking.

"I'd forgotten how much I hate space travel,"
said Lance.

"I thought I told you to Shut. It. Off,"
growled Amy.

Bus driver C.J. yelled, "Flat tire! Hold tight!"

He pulled off onto the shoulder, which was a little scary and really bumpy, especially with no seat belts, and seats that had absolutely zero cushion. This time we were all throwing our hands up and going, "Wah!" like Dwight had been doing all morning, but for real.

"SETTLE DOWN! Just sit still! Keep it cool!" Ms. Rabbski was hollering.

C.J. got out. Then got back on.

He said, "Yep."

Then he called somebody on his phone. Then talked into a little microphone he had. Then got back on the phone. We were all waiting to hear what he was going say.

Finally:

C.J.:   It's gonna be an hour and a half!

Rabbski: Can one of the other buses pick us up?

C.J.:   No, they're long gone. They passed us
           an hour ago. They're almost ready to

THIS IS WHY WE USE TANK TREADS

THE SCOOBY BUS

YEP!

pull off for supper at the Harrisonburg McDonald's.

Me (Mike) and just about every other kid on the bus: What about OUR supper?

Rabbski: We are just going to have to wait . . . [And then she talked for five minutes about how she didn't want to hear the words "supper" or "bathroom" until we were under way again. I thought about the Sasquatch sticks sitting in my bag . . . on one of those OTHER buses, because Mr. Howell wouldn't let us get our stuff. Then I remembered that Dwight had been carrying his bag of Fruit Roll-Ups with him through the museum, turning them into Yoda as needed.]

Me (Mike): Dwight, do you have any more Fruit Roll-Ups?

Dwight: It's Captain Dwight, and I have one left, but I'm saving it for Yoda-related emergencies.

Amy: Don't tell me you ate that whole bag of Fruit Roll-Ups!

Dwight: Purple.

The same thing was true all around the bus. Most of the snacks had either been eaten already or had been left on the other bus.

We were stranded with no food . . . For an hour and a half . . . and it was getting dark . . . and we all hated each other . . .

Misery . . .

Gloom . . .

Whining . . .

Tommy saying, "Shut UP, Harvey . . ."

And then, after about a parsec and a half of waiting, Quavondo goes: "Now I see! This is what the ice cream is for! It's like the Cheetos all over again."

He got up and started handing out packs of astronaut ice cream from his big bag.

Everybody was stretching their hands out for a pack, and he walked down the aisle like the Easter Bunny handing out Cadbury eggs.

There were EXACTLY enough packs to give one to everybody on the bus . . . including the chaperones and C.J. the bus driver.

Harvey was the only person who didn't want any.

Harvey/Pickletine: Oh, I assure you . . . it is quite disgusting . . . I have foreseen—

Quavondo: [Cutting him off and grabbing the ice cream back.] This is perfect! There's one extra pack! I can give it to my sister! I'm saved!!!!!

UH? DUDE? I WAS STILL TALKING?

[I'm not sure what the ice cream would have tasted like normally. Maybe if you took it home and ate it by yourself, sitting on the couch, it wouldn't be so good. But there on the bus, when we were all so hungry and so, so bored, it was like . . . well, like Cadbury eggs or something.]

Lance: Oh, My Nox! It's disgustingly delicious!

Kellen: Use a lot of saliva and it sort of turns back into ice cream!

Rhondella: Ew!

Dwight: Purrrrrple . . .

Tommy: I'm saving some of the strawberry and

SURE BEATS THOSE HEALTH-SICLES BACK AT SCHOOL!

YEAH, BUT I WISH THEY HAD MY FAVORITE FLAVOR . . . EWOK.

chocolate parts to make Freeze-Dried
Darth Maul!

[And then came the most shocking moment of all
. . .]

Howell: Quavondo, I misjudged you, sir. You
have my apology and my thanks for this
delicious treat! Would anyone care to
join me in showing our appreciation to
Quavondo?

Everybody: THANKS, QUAVONDO!!!!

Then Jen said, "Let's do a cheer, Piper!"
She and Piper jumped up and did one of those
little semi-disco dances that cheerleaders do.

"Astronaut ice cream!
It's a freeze-dried delight!
Thank you, Amy, Mike, and Dwight!
Astronaut ice cream!
It's shaped like blocks!
Give a big cheer because Quavondo rocks!"

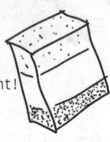

AND THEN . . .

Are you ready for this? Because this is going to show that Origami Yoda was right about "field trip of destiny" and all that stuff.

Jen came over and kissed Quavondo on the cheek. OH GOOD GRIEF!

Then she went back and we heard her tell Piper, "I couldn't help it! He's SO cute!"

And Quavondo's big ears turned redder and redder and popped off his head and we had to crawl around on the floor of the bus looking for them. (Not really.)

"Well, was that worth a hundred and fifty bucks?" I asked.

". . . yes . . . ," Quavondo wheezed.

I told you: When Origami Yoda says "Must," he means MUST!

AGREE I MUST!

Harvey's Comment

The official NASA website says that freeze-dried ice cream was only used the first time a crew of astronauts went into space! (Apollo 7.) After that,

BLECH!

they didn't even bother to take it along! Probably because it's completely awful. But the gift shops just keep on selling it and selling it. Now if you

[Rest of comment deleted]

My Comment: I had to listen to Harvey's "official" narnar for the next half hour, and there is no way I'm putting it all in the case file. If anyone wants to know, they can Google it.

There's a big difference between this event and the Cheetos event. With the Cheetos, Quavondo was pretending to be generous and gave away Cheetos so that he could get rid of his embarrassing nickname, Cheeto Hog.

This time, he wasn't pretending. He could have just sat there and said nothing and taken all twenty-eight packs home with him. Instead, he gave them away! What a nice guy! Kit Fisto would be proud!

GEEZ, YOU'D NEED A LIGHTSABER TO CUT THIS PIECE OF OWL!

I THINK I JUST BROKE A TOOTH!

TOMMY

BIGGIE-SIZE
MY COMBOS!

BY TOMMY

After the ice cream, people didn't seem to hate each other quite as much. And Rabbski and Howell weren't quite so strict, so we started joking around some again, and I even got to talk diagonally across the aisle to Sara without getting yelled at. (Kellen, how about a new seating chart?)

Finally, the tow truck came and we all got off and stood in the grass while it hoisted the bus up and put on a new tire.

It only took a few minutes and then we were

JABBA
THE
FLATT
↓

YOU MAY TIRE WHEN READY...

GRAND MOFF TIREKIN →

back on the bus and the bus was back on the road.

Rabbski: C.J., I don't think this group is going to last all the way to the Harrisonburg McDonald's. Do you know if there's one coming up sooner?

Dwight: [Yelling from the back of the bus.] There's a Wendy's at Exit 283!

C.J.: That's about fifteen minutes away.

Rabbski: [Getting out her cell phone.] Oh, okay. I'll look that up on Google and see if I can find their phone—

Dwight: 540 J-J-K B-E-E-F!

Rabbski: Oh! Well, thank you, Dwight. I'm going to call ahead to the restaurant and order our food now so it's ready when we get there. To keep it simple, I'm going to order everyone a double cheeseburger combo.

One of Mrs. Porterfield's kids: I am SO hungry! Can you make them Biggie-size combos?

Rabbski: Uh, does anyone know how much it costs to do that?

The entire back of the bus: THIRTY-NINE CENTS!!!!!!!!!

Rabbski: Oooookay . . . Sure, we can do that.

Sara: Excuse me, Ms. Rabbski? Quavondo's a vegetarian.

Quavondo: I'll make an exception this one time!!! I'd hate to cause a problem!

Quavondo's stomach: MEAT! MEAT! I LOVE MEAT!!!!!!!!!!

[I'm just guessing that's what his stomach said.]

But then Quavondo remembered that he didn't have any money left!

"Dude! How are we going to pay for our Biggie-size double cheeseburger combos?" he asked Mike in a panic. "We spent all our money!"

"Keep calm," said Mike, "and trust Fruitigami Yoda."

"Trust him?" sneered Harvey/Emperor

Pickletine. "You're going to have to EAT him!"

And then Rabbski finished her phone call and announced that she was just going to pay for it with her credit card and figure out how much everybody owed later.

"I told you," said Mike. "Fruitigami Yoda thinks of everything!"

And then pretty soon we were pulling off the interstate into Wendy's.

Harvey's Comment

I wanted to go to McDonalds.

My Comment: Yeah, I heard. (About a million times.) But I think Wendy's was ... our destiny.

157

AW, AREN'T THEY JUST ADORWABLE?

TOMMY + SARA

WENDY'S

BY TOMMY

When we got into Wendy's, they were just finishing bagging up our orders.

"Here you are," said the manager. "Twenty-seven Biggie-size double cheeseburger value meals and one Kids' Meal."

"I didn't order a Kids' Meal," said Rabbski.

"Oh, I could have sworn you said . . . ," started the manager.

"Thank you very much," said Dwight, grabbing the Kids' Meal bag and going off to sit under a table.

"Okeydokey then," said Ms. Rabbski, and
she handed over her credit card.

"Oh, My Nox!" said Lance. "Listen!"

We listened. And you could hear "Kiss This
Kiss" playing over the restaurant's speakers.

KISS
THIS
KISS

ROXY
DIAMOND

"They're playing our song," he said to Amy.

"Hmmmph," said Amy. But it was less icy
than the previous fifty "Hmmmph"s she had
given him.

I FINALLY got to sit down next to Sara,
and we sat so close that our shoulders were
touching, and it was nice . . . until Ms.
Rabbski and Mr. Howell sat down at our table,
then we scooted apart a little bit.

Mr. Howell said, "Lougene, I just remembered
. . . I checked my voice mail earlier and I
got the weirdest message. They wanted me to
get you to call the school about the Standards
tests. Sorry, it slipped my mind during all
the . . . hubbub."

"Don't worry, I got the same message . . .
about eighteen times," she said.

18

"Trouble?"

"Oh, no," said Rabbski, "probably just the Edu-Fun man calling. I'll be sure to call him back first thing tomorrow."

And she giggled.

"Or maybe first thing next week," she said, and giggled again.

"When are we supposed to take the stupid tests, anyway?" Sara asked.

"Today," answered Rabbski.

"Wait, what?" said everybody who heard her.

"Didn't you know?" asked Ms. Rabbski. "Today was seventh-grade Core Standards test day. An Edu-Fun testing specialist came today with the tests in sealed cartons. And several test supervisors came from the central office, too. Testing began exactly at nine fifteen. How did you do?"

Now everybody was listening and basically thinking: "WHUT THE HUTT?"

"We weren't there!" said Mike. "We were on a bus with you."

"You were? I hope you had number-two pencils and carefully shaded in the bubbles!"

"Uh, no?" said Jen. "We didn't do any of that!"

"We're on a field trip! The WHOLE seventh grade is on the field trip!" said Lance.

"Really?" asked Rabbski. "So none of you took the test? Oh, dearie me! What a terrible mix-'em-up!"

We all just sat there for a minute, trying to figure out what on earth she was talking about. And Ms. Rabbski giggled some more, soon joined by Mrs. Porterfield.

> SNORT!

"Oh, I just hate to think about that poor Edu-Fun testing specialist walking around and around the school with his sealed cartons and his bubble sheets, trying to find a seventh grader!" said Mrs. Porterfield.

AND SHE AND MS. RABBSKI KEPT ON GIGGLING.

And then something even more unbelievable happened!

MISTER. HOWELL. GIGGLED.

NOT EVEN AN EVIL CHUCKLE! A REAL GIGGLE!

HEE HEE

161

We just stared.

And then . . .

Mr. Howell: I love you.

Ms. Rabbski: I know.

And then . . .

"Let's Twist Again"!

It was coming from the speakers in the ceiling. They had been playing nothing but cruddy pop junk like "Kiss This Kiss" the whole time we were in there.

And now they were playing:

"Yeah, let's twist again,
Like we did last year!"

"NO! No way!" yelled Harvey. But it was really happening.

NObbOOOOOOd!

"Do you remember when
Things were really hummin'?

Yeah, let's twist again,
Twistin' time is here!"

It wasn't the same song from Fun Night. That was just "The Twist." This song was saying, "Let's twist again," but it sounded like basically the exact same music with new words. But still really old.

"Would you like to dance, Lougene?" asked Mr. Howell.

"I thought you'd never ask," said Ms. Rabbski.

They got up and started twisting.

So WE got up and started twisting!

Me and Sara, of course. But also Lance and Amy, thank goodness. And . . . Kellen and Cassie? What??? And Jen and Quavondo! WHAT???? And Dwight and Mrs. Porterfield (who could REALLY twist!). And even the kids who hadn't twisted with us last year figured it out pretty quick.

It was so stooky, everybody was doing it!

Well, except for Rhondella, who was rolling her eyes, and Harvey, who was busy harassing Dwight: "Did you get them to play this?"

Dwight just held up Fruitigami Yoda. "Twist you must!"

But Harvey wouldn't do it. All he would do was gripe and make accusations, and then he went up to ask the manager if Dwight had arranged the whole thing.

But the rest of us twisted, and since twisting gets old after forty-five seconds, we invented new moves, and Lance fell over and got ketchup in his hair and Amy fussed over him with a napkin, and Sara kept smiling at me, and . . . it was stooky, what else can I say?

And by the time the song was over and Ms. Rabbski was telling everybody to use the bathroom now because it was going to be a LONG time before we stopped again, everybody was friends again—or, in some cases, MORE than friends again, or maybe just maybe in some other cases, MORE than friends for the first time!

OH, POOR LAN-LAN.

"LAN LAN" KETCHUP

I HAVE A BAD FEELING ABOUT THIS . . .

164

SPITTLE

FOAM

NARNAR

HARVEY'S COMMENT

BY TOMMY

Tommy's note: This is not a normal Harvey comment that he wrote down. This is a BRIEF excerpt of the ENDLESS narnar that began immediately after the song ended.

"No way! Just no way! There is no way that really happened, and don't try to tell me that Paperwad Yoda—excuse me, Fruitwad Yoda—made 'The Twist' play with the Force. That's just dumb. Dwight faked it the first time and he faked it this time. I just have to figure out how!"

GUIDE TO HARVEYISMS:

PAPERWAD YODA

FRUITWAD YODA

MY PRETTY BECCARY!™

At first, I argued with him. "How could he have done that? He was busy playing with his Kids' Meal toy the whole time!"

But soon, I just wanted the conversation to end, so I stopped arguing and just tried to ignore him. NOT EASY!

"Did you notice that the volume went up when 'The Twist' started playing? That proves that someone was in the back, fiddling with the controls. I don't care what the manager said about them not having any control over it. That's bantha dung! Dwight probably paid them to play it, and then paid them not to tell me. And then—"

And it didn't stop there. Harvey just couldn't turn it off. The only time he'd stop was to give Pickletine a chance to say I had a "pitiful brain" or something like that. Then Harvey would get right back into it. And not just what happened at Wendy's, and not just what happened at the museum, but everything that had happened since Origami Yoda first

RUSH IN FOOLS DO!

166

showed up: the pre-eaten weiner, the snot trooper, the first time "The Twist" played.

It was like he had forgotten all the good stuff. I mean, it was just a few weeks ago that we had that awesome crab soccer game. Not to mention defeating Professor FunTime.

That's when I realized for sure that Mike was right about Pickletine. Whether he was really using the Dark Side of the Force or whether he just reminded Harvey to be angry, he was certainly making this trip miserable.

For once, Harvey wasn't shouting. If he had done that, Mr. Howell would have come back and yelled at us. No, this was muttering and griping and whining and hissing, and it went on for the next hour or so on the bus.

"Just. Let. It. GO!!!!" I begged.

But he wouldn't. He couldn't.

"I think the bus driver was in on it! He tricked Rabbski into going to Wendy's!"

"By having a flat tire on purpose?"

"No, but he may have said something like—"

HEH
HEH
HEH!

"Look, Harvey, I don't care anymore. It doesn't matter. It happened. And it was fun! At least for the rest of us it was fun!"

"Yeah, maybe one of YOU did it! Why didn't I think of that? I asked the manager if Dwight had done it. But it could have been any of you treacherous Jedi traitors!"

By the end of that sentence he was talking like Palpatine again and shaking the now totally dried up wrinkle-pickle in my face.

SHRIV-
ELED

I was losing my mind . . .

And then all of a sudden, Rhondella came sneaking down the aisle to our seat.

"Sara wants to see you a minute."

It was dark enough now that I could easily slip up the aisle without Rabbski and Howell noticing. They were busy blabbing to each other anyway.

I sort of crawl-walked up there and sat next to her.

She put her finger to her lips and then gestured for me to lean close.

SKIP THE
NEXT PAGE!

168

She whispered in my ear:

"that was amazing."

"what? harvey?"

"no, 'the twist'! at wendy's."

"oh, yeah, absolutely . . ."

"is harvey driving you nuts back there?"

"yes."

"well, here's something to make you feel better."

And she kissed me.

On the lips.

And I definitely felt better. But also weirder. Weirder than anything. A LOT weirder than the time my dad drove over the fire hydrant. That was nothing compared to this.

"you better go back to your seat now before you get caught."

"okay."

I crept back down the aisle to where Rhondella was sitting with Harvey.

"well?" she whispered.

And she had that old Rhondella smirky-smile

RED ALERT!

DON'T DRAW IT! PLEASE DON'T DRAW IT!

WELL . . . IT'S OVER. THANKS FOR NOT DRAWING IT!!

DON'T WORRY, DUDE! I WOULDN'T DRAW THAT FOR 100 BUCKS

I hadn't seen in a long time. She had known Sara was going to kiss me. It was all part of a plan. I was aware that my ears were turning as red as Quavondo's had—probably my whole face, too—but it was hopefully dark enough so it didn't matter. Hopefully.

I didn't say anything.

But she whispered "mmm-hmmmm, I know what just happened."

And the way she said it made it clear to everybody nearby what had just happened.

"you can have harvey back now," she whispered. "he's in a great mood . . ."

She went back up to her seat.

And I sat down with Harvey again.

And I was thinking about a million things but mostly about one thing and it was great and the field trip was everything Origami Yoda had promised and . . .

KA . . .

BY TOMMY

. . . then . . .

POW!

BY TOMMY

Harvey punched me in the nose.

SEE BELOW
↓

OWWW!!!!!!!

BY TOMMY

Me: OWWW!!!!!!!!!

TOMMY + HIS "BUS BUDDY"

BLOOD ON THE BUS

BY TOMMY

A LOT of things all happened at exactly the same time.

We're really going to have to go into SUPER SLO-MO here, starting with the millisecond after I hollered, "OWWW!!!!!!!"

"WHAT ON EARTH IS GOING ON BACK THERE?" yells Rabbski.

She and Howell both jump up and start down the aisle toward us. I can't see them, of course . . . just giant shadows of student-crushing authority lumbering toward me! And

this isn't a long bus, so it isn't going to take long!

The driver turns the lights on at this point.

I suddenly see all these faces looking at me over the seat backs.

What they see is me with my hands over my face and blood dripping everywhere!

I turn to glare at Harvey. Maybe he's about to hit me again . . . but actually he's frozen. He looks like someone has punched him, too.

"I—" he stammers.

Rabbski is getting closer . . .

And that's when I realize that I now have the power to destroy Harvey and his obnoxious pickle puppet! In another second, when Rabbski and Howell reach the back of the bus, all I have to do is tell them what happened, and Harvey will be in the biggest trouble of his life!

Ms. Rabbski will switch back to full

Principal Rabbski mode! She'll grill Harvey, fill out incident reports, call in his parents— no, wait, his parents will be waiting at the school parking lot . . . They'll hear all about this tonight! Whatever is left of him after Rabbski has done her job, they'll then tear apart!

And what then? Punishment! ISS! Suspension! Expulsion? Won't that serve him right? If HE's the one who ends up at the hideous CREF reform school?

His fate is in my hands! In fact, I probably won't even need to say a word, just point at Harvey.

The milliseconds of slo-mo are almost over. Rabbski and Howell are close enough to see all the blood now.

"Get the first-aid kit from up front," Rabbski says, and Howell rushes back the other way.

And suddenly, Yoda is there . . . Dwight is stretched over two seat backs, shoving

NO HARVEY?

him practically in my face. It looks good, despite being made of a Fruit Roll-Up. Dwight must have spent a long time folding this one . . . all the folds, all the wrinkles are there. . . . just like the real Origami Yoda.

"Search your—"

"DWIGHT! Put that away! NOW!" shouts Rabbski.

But I know what he was trying to say: "Search your feelings, Tommy."

So I do.

I think sometimes I understand Harvey more than I let on. And I don't think he's a bad guy, he just doesn't know how to deal with people.

But then again . . . neither does Dwight, really, without Origami Yoda's help.

And then again, the rest of us need Origami Yoda's help, too.

And so does Harvey. But he refuses to listen. Or worse, he ends up listening to Darth Paper or Pickletine.

But even after all the obnoxious Dark Side nonsense we've had to listen to on this trip, here's Origami Yoda still trying to help him by asking me to search my feelings.

And now my feelings tell me to think about Harvey's feelings.

Harvey did have a pretty lousy day. Some of that was his own fault, but not all of it. After all, my day would have been pretty cruddy, too, if it wasn't for that kiss from Sara. And Harvey didn't get something like that, and—

And that's when I realize that Harvey is in love with Sara, too. It seems so obvious now when I think about some of the things he's said and the comments he made on her files and stuff he's done.

That's why he's been mad all day. All year? And that's why "The Twist" made him so mad. Both times!

And then, to see me sneak up there and get

WOAH! SARA? I DID NOT SEE THAT COMING!!!

ARE YOU KIDDING? IT'S BEEN OBVIOUS FOR THE LAST 3 CASE FILES!

a kiss after all the defeats and problems he had this trip, I can see why he gave in to the Dark Side.

And why I needed to pull him back to the, uh, Light Side? Is that the opposite of the Dark Side? Is there a name for it? I'll have to look it up on—

"What happened here?" demanded Rabbski.

"I twibbed," I said.

"Tripped? What were you doing out of your seat!"

"I snubbked bhup btoo see Sabwa. Ibt bwas dark abnd—"

"HMMMPPHHH!" she said, and it was a mad "Hmmmpphhh," but it wasn't THAT mad.

"All right, we'll go into that later. Let's try to stop the bleeding right now."

And Mr. Howell brought the first-aid kit and they shoved cotton up my nose and put on gloves and wiped up the blood. And I remember thinking that if Mr. Good Clean Fun was still

A LITTLE MORE!

ANTI-EVERYTHING

our chaperone, he would have had to sanitize the entire bus.

And then Rabbski fussed at Dwight for having Origami Yoda . . . but he had popped it into his mouth and was trying to swallow it.

"I don't feel good," he said.

And then he barfed up all the Fruit Roll-Ups and the astronaut ice cream and his happy meal . . . onto Kellen's pants.

AFTER
AFTER

And if Mr. Good Clean Fun had seen that, he would have jumped out the window.

And the driver stopped at a rest stop so we could get everything cleaned up.

And while we were walking back from the little building to the bus, Sara made a big deal about me being hurt and kissed me on the nose and said, "All better?"

And Mike and Kellen made gagging noises, but who cares?

And then the driver turned the lights out again.

And we rode on home in the dark.

WHAT? MORE KISSING?

THIS IS AN OUTRAGE!

And finally, like, fifty miles later, Harvey said he was sorry.

"I was mad because you and Sara . . . Because I've always— You know."

"Yeah. I do now."

"And then the game and the airplane and—"

"Yeah."

"It just felt like everybody was against me all day."

Of course I didn't have Foldy-Wan with me, but somehow I felt some of that wisdom right then.

"No," I told Harvey, "it was Pickletine that was against you."

"Definitely," he said. Then Harvey pulled Pickletine out of his sweatshirt and smooshed it up into a black, sour-smelling paperwad.

EMPEROR PALPERWAD!

"It was a good fold, though," I said. "With brown paper it would make a good Jedi robe."

"Hrmmm," he grunted.

And later he said, "Why didn't you tell on me?"

And I couldn't explain it, so I just said, "Fruitigami Yoda."

"Yeah," he said. "I guess so."

And later he said, "Thanks."

And somehow, before we got back to the school, he and me and Kellen and Mike were having a big argument about whether Yoda was better as a puppet or as computer animation.

FOR THE LAST TIME, WOULD YOU PLEASE BE QUIET!

And Lance tried to get in on it, but he got too loud and Ms. Rabbski turned around and hollered at us.

And then we were back and our parents were there and the field trip was over.

Well, not totally over: One very odd thing happened before we all left. Dwight went over to Harvey and whispered in his ear. And Harvey whispered in Dwight's ear. And back and forth a few times.

And then Harvey said, "May the Force be with you, Master Yoda . . . and you, too, Captain Dwight." But then he walked over to me and said, "I know something you don't know."

Harvey's Comment

Actually, I know A LOT of things you don't know! ←

My Comment: That's your comment?? After everything
we went through? The complaining, the griping, the
Pickletine-ing, and the other thing-ing? That's your
comment????

  I'm going to give you another chance for a better
comment.

Harvey's Second-
Chance Comment

You're right, Tommy. I sincerely apologize for any and ←
all complaining, griping, and Pickletine-ing, and, yes, I
am very, very sorry for the other thing. Really!
  However . . . I still know something you don't know!

THE EMPTY TREASURE CHEST

THE DAY AFTER
THE FIELD TRIP

BY TOMMY

Okay, so the field trip had turned out pretty good . . . maybe.

Yes, there was still a big maybe hanging over us! Were our parents going to find out about the paper airplane incident?

If they didn't find out, then, yes, the field trip was stooky.

If they did find out, then . . . DOOM!!!!!!

When the buses had dropped us off the night before, none of the chaperones had said anything to our parents about anything. And

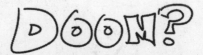

now that we were back at school, we were all hoping that everyone would forget about it and be ready to move on.

But we had forgotten one thing. It might seem tiny, but it's like the tiny clue in a detective show that has almost nothing to do with anything but it's enough to make the detective raise an eyebrow and then the criminal gets sent to prison forever.

In this case, that one thing was Miss Bauer's Treasure Hunt worksheets.

You might say, "After all that crazy business, who cares about a Treasure Hunt worksheet?"

Well, Miss Bauer cares about Treasure Hunt worksheets! It turns out that we needed to turn them in for a grade.

Of course, we didn't have them anymore. And everybody else filled theirs in yesterday while on the trip, so we couldn't make copies of those.

Obviously, we couldn't ask Miss Bauer for

DON'T EVEN ASK!

replacement copies without going into details that would be better not to bring up. (Not even Mr. Howell realized that we had used our worksheets to make the airplanes.)

So we were all set up to get an F on the easiest assignment of the year—and, frankly, my grade in Bauer's class was already in trouble.

But, still, that's not THAT big of a deal, right?

Wrong, because here's how it becomes a big deal. When you get an F on an assignment, Miss Bauer sends a "neon note" home to your parents. (They're printed on neon paper.)

Neon notes have to be signed by your parents. So you show it to them, and next thing you know, they're asking a bunch of questions. And then . . . the truth comes out!

That is the LAST thing any of us needed!

But the whole thing could be avoided if we could just get blank copies of the worksheet.

We could fill it out in two minutes and be saved!

With about twenty minutes before the homeroom bell, me, Lance, and Kellen were concerned but not panicking yet. Once Dwight showed up, we could just ask Origami Yoda what to do about it.

Harvey just kept saying, "Maybe Origami Yoda isn't coming . . ."

But he had to be coming! Sara, who rides Dwight's bus, said Dwight had been on the bus. So he WAS at school, he must have just gotten distracted . . . or lost.

A search party was formed. Mike, Quavondo, and Sara all agreed to help us look, even though they already had their (unfortunately filled-out) worksheets.

Harvey wouldn't go. He needed a worksheet as much as any of us, but he refused to look for Dwight.

"You might find Dwight, but I don't think you're going to find Origami Yoda," he said.

"Uh, Harvey, I thought you decided to start being nice after what happened on the bus last night?"

"I AM being nice. I'm trying to save you the trouble of finding Dwight when he won't be able to help you."

NICE?

"ARRRGH!" I said, and stomped off.

I found Dwight down in hallway B, talking to Cody C. They were deep in discussion about that clock-maker exhibit Dwight had seen on the trip.

"Sorry to interrupt, guys, but I NEED to ask Origami Yoda a question."

"I don't have him," said Dwight, like THAT was no big deal.

"What? Did you leave him at home?"

"No."

"YOU LOST HIM????"

"No."

ABSENT?

"Then where is he??????"

I had a bad feeling about this! Maybe Harvey was right!

"He left."

"What do you mean he left?"

"He told me to give you something, though."

He pulled out an Origami Yoda made from white paper.

"Thank Jar Jar!" I shouted. "Origami Yoda, what should we do about the worksheets?"

Origami Yoda didn't say anything. Dwight and Cody C. looked at me like I was nuts.

"Please, Yoda! What should we do about the worksheets?" I begged.

"Uh, Tommy? Why are you yelling at a piece of paper?" asked Cody C.

"Because we always ask Origami Yoda questions," I shouted.

"This isn't Origami Yoda," said Dwight. "This is a Yoda made using origami. Specifically, it's the Force Ghost Yoda from *Return of the Jedi*."

"I love that movie," said Cody C.

"Me, too," said Dwight. "Have you read the book version?"

FORCE GHOST ORIGAMI YODA →

"No, is that good?"

"Well—"

"Dwight!" I yelled. "Dude, I need your help here. I'm running out of time! Why won't Origami Yoda help me?"

"Aren't you listening?" asked Cody C. "Origami Yoda is not here. He left. But before he left, he told Dwight to make you this Force Ghost Yoda."

"I heard all that!" I snapped. "It's not helping!!! Would you please tell me—"

I stopped. Because I had just realized what the ghost Yoda was made out of. Dwight had folded it out of his FIELD TRIP WORKSHEET! Which he had never filled in!!!

"I'll bring this right back!" I told him.

I raced to the library, just praying that Rabbski wasn't lurking about to nail me for running in the hall.

CREASED
+
WRINKLED,
BUT BLANK!

The other guys were already there.

"We didn't find him," said Kellen.

"I DID! Long story. Here's the worksheet."

OUR HERO AGAIN!

I had unfolded it as I ran. Kellen grabbed it, ran up to Mrs. Calhoun, and begged her to make copies. She did. (She's nice!)

The homeroom bell rang. But that was fine. We had what we needed.

In homeroom, I gave Dwight his copy of the worksheet back and recommended that he get it done. Instead of playing pencil-flick games, we sat down and filled out all the squares. One of the questions was "What was the most important historical artifact you saw in a museum?"

EASY! "Bell X-1!!!!"

Dwight put some ridiculously long answer about the clock-maker guy. In fact, he spent most of homeroom on that one question. His answer wrapped around to the back of the paper.

When I finished, I finally relaxed. Origami Yoda had saved us yet again.

"So, Dwight," I said. "Now will you tell me what's going on with Origami Yoda?"

"I already did."

"But I need the whole story."

"Oh, would you like me to write something for your case file?"

WOULD I LIKE HIM TO WRITE SOMETHING FOR THE CASE FILE????????

I have been begging him to write something since the very first case file! I mean, Dwight is the only one who actually really knows what's going on! Even if he acts like he doesn't!

"Yes! Please!!!!"

"Okay," said Dwight. And he pulled out a notebook and started writing it up right there!

"At last," I thought, "I'm going to get the real answers to all the questions!" Is Origami Yoda real? Is he using the Force? How does he know so much? Why is he helping us in the first place? And on and on . . .

Did I get the answers? Well . . . read it yourself and find out.

THE ANSWER BY DWIGHT

Of course I was right! Why do you always doubt me? I told you I knew something you didn't know! But I couldn't tell you everything, because when Dwight told me what was going to happen, he told me it was a secret. So . . . I WAS being nice!

My Comment: Good grief . . . Well, I guess the secret is out now.

ARE YOU GUYS STILL LOOKING FOR THAT WORKSHEET? I FOUND ONE IN THE TRASH . . . IT'S KINDA COVERED IN BAKED BEANS, THOUGH. I FIND A LOT OF WEIRD STUFF THAT'S COVERED IN BAKED BEANS, ACTUALLY . . .

LUNCHMAN JEFF'S COMMENT

ORIGAMI YODA AND THE MAIL-LENNIUM FALCON

BY DWIGHT ➩FINALLY!

Stardate: 387

Planet: Earth

System: Zynamon 5 (known locally as the Solar System)

Outside temperature: 61 degrees

Who: Dwight, aka Sherlock Dwight, aka the Magic Squirrel of Silent Movie Fame, formerly Captain Dwight

Best friend: Caroline →

Favorite color: Orange

Last night: Returned from field trip late. (See separate report for details on clock-making exhibit and Wendy's Kids' Meal.)

Thanked Mom for ride home and apologized again for delays. Went straight to bedroom to talk with Origami Yoda.

"Met Captain Micah, did you?" he asked.

"Yes, he's cool. But as you predicted, he does need your help."

"Hrmm . . . yes . . . as I feared it is. His address? Get it you did?"

"Yes."

Pulled out paper. Some worksheet I had not filled out. But important information was safely written on the back: the address of Captain Micah.

"Prepare Mail-lennium Falcon you must."

"I don't want to."

"Hrmm . . . ," said Origami Yoda. "Sad I am also that this day has come. But it must be."

"Must?"

"Must, my friend . . . must."

So I got an envelope and I wrote Micah's address on it.

"I don't have any stamps. Should I ask Mom?"

"Stamps I need not. But window a little bit open you must leave it."

I opened the window. (My mom doesn't have them nailed shut anymore).

"Cry you need not, but if you do, then a tissue you should use, not shirtsleeve."

"Okay."

"Alone you will not be. Not now. Caroline you will still have. And Tommy and Kellen and Sara and the others. Harvey, too."

"But what about them? They need you, too!"

"Hrmm . . . Yes. Impatient, reckless they are. A Force Ghost Yoda you must fold them tomorrow. A little more help they need. After that . . . the Force will be with them."

And then he walked over to the Mail-lennium Falcon.

"And the Force will be with you, too, Dwight . . . Always."

Then he climbed into the Mail-lennium Falcon and it flew out the window.

I closed the window and went to bed.

Harvey's Comment

I, **Harvey Cunningham,** BELIEVE that everything happened just the way Dwight said it did.

Farewell, origami Yoda, and may the force be with you, too.

My Comment: I don't know what to say.

I know this will make ME sound like Harvey, but . . . I CAN'T believe it.

I don't want to believe it.

Plus, it's crazy. How could Origami Yoda walk? He doesn't even have feet?

I've asked Dwight that question and a million more, but all he'll say now is "Purple." The only question he does answer is when I ask him if Origami Yoda is coming back. And then he says, "I don't know," and he looks so sad that I think he really doesn't know.

I've asked him to fold emergency Yodas and he does,

PURPLE!

but they don't have anything to say.

Foldy-Wan Kenobi doesn't have anything to say, either. None of our puppets do. I mean, we can force them to say something, but that's not really the same. (Actually, Remi claims that her Ewoks still say "Yub nub" on their own. But that doesn't exactly help solve our various problems, does it?)

Sara said that maybe it's like in "Return of the Jedi," how Luke didn't really need Yoda anymore. Maybe after the various things that happened on the field trip—like Harvey crumpling up the Emperor and Mr. Howell telling Ms. Rabbski that he loved her and Sara and I . . . you know—maybe after all that, we don't need Origami Yoda anymore.

Maybe, but I don't buy it. We still have plenty of problems. And I don't think Sara realizes just how clueless we are about stuff and how much dumb stuff I would have done without his advice. Man, just think how much Origami Yoda has done for us in the last year . . .

DWIGHT

• STILL DWIGHT, BUT NOW
WE UNDERSTAND HIM (SOMETIMES)

And then think about NEXT year! The eighth grade! And then high school! And who knows what all else is going to happen to us . . . or what kind of messes we're going to get into.

We totally need Yoda's help for all that!!!!!

And then there's another thing . . .

If Origami Yoda is gone, then does that mean no more case files?

Is this . . . the end?

HIGH SCHOOL?
REAL DATES? JOBS?
EXAMS? DRIVER'S ED?????

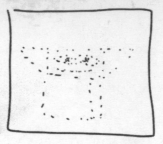

FORCE GHOST YODA

BY TOMMY

Miss Bauer handed back our worksheets.

I asked Dwight if I could see his.

Yes, it had an address scribbled on the back. But I couldn't read it, and Dwight didn't really seem sure what it said anymore, either. We had no way to contact the kid and tell him to send Origami Yoda back!

Then I asked Dwight if he would refold it into Force Ghost Yoda for me.

He did.

And when he gave it back to me, I asked it, "Is this the end?"

It didn't talk, exactly. Not like Origami Yoda did. But it was almost like I could hear Force Ghost Origami Yoda the way Luke could hear Force Ghost Obi-Wan.

And Force Ghost Yoda was saying, "Search your feelings."

And I did.

And then I was sure.

Origami Yoda may not come back right away. Maybe not this year. Maybe not for years. Not until we REALLY, REALLY, REALLY need him. I don't know when that will be or how we will tell him or if he will just know or if he is even really gone or is maybe just lost in Dwight's room somewhere and one day Dwight will find him and say he came back or maybe he really did fly away to see that kid and the kid will send him back.

I have no idea. And normally when I have no idea about something, I ask Origami Yoda. BUT I CAN'T!!!!!!!

But I am sure of one thing:

"The end this is not!"

EMPEROR PICKLETINE

INSTRUCTIONS BY HARVEY
DRAWN BY KELLEN!! PICKLE COURTESY OF LUNCHMAN JEFF

① FOLD BOTH CORNERS DOWN . . .

② MAKE SURE THEY OVERLAP A BIT AT POINT Ⓐ

③ FOLD BACK NOTE: FOLD GOES THRU POINT Ⓐ

④ FLIP OVER

⑤ FOLD SIDES BACK

⑥ FLIP LOOKS LIKE A VERY TALL JEDI OR SITH . . .

HOW TO MAKE A FACE . . .

① FIND TWO EVIL PICKLE SLICES

② CUT EYEBROWS + EVIL SMILE FROM ONE

③ CUT A PIECE OF RED CANDY TO MAKE EVIL EYES. JELLY BEANS, RED HOTS, GUM, ETC . . .

④ ARRANGE PIECES ON PICKLE

OR... JUST DRAW A NASTY FACE ON A GREEN CIRCLE

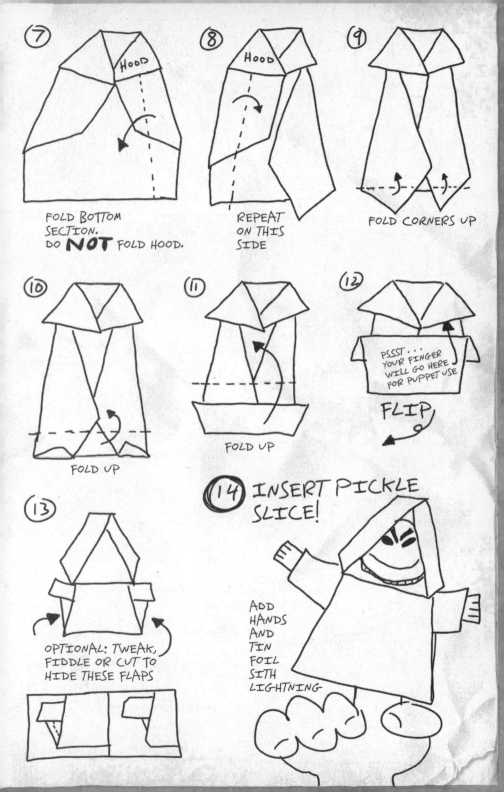

⑦ **HOOD**

FOLD BOTTOM
SECTION.
DO **NOT** FOLD HOOD.

⑧ **HOOD**

REPEAT
ON THIS
SIDE

⑨

FOLD CORNERS UP

⑩

FOLD UP

⑪

FOLD UP

⑫

PSSST...
YOUR FINGER
WILL GO HERE
FOR PUPPET USE

FLIP

⑬

OPTIONAL: TWEAK,
FIDDLE OR CUT TO
HIDE THESE FLAPS

⑭ INSERT PICKLE
SLICE!

ADD
HANDS
AND
TIN
FOIL
SITH
LIGHTNING

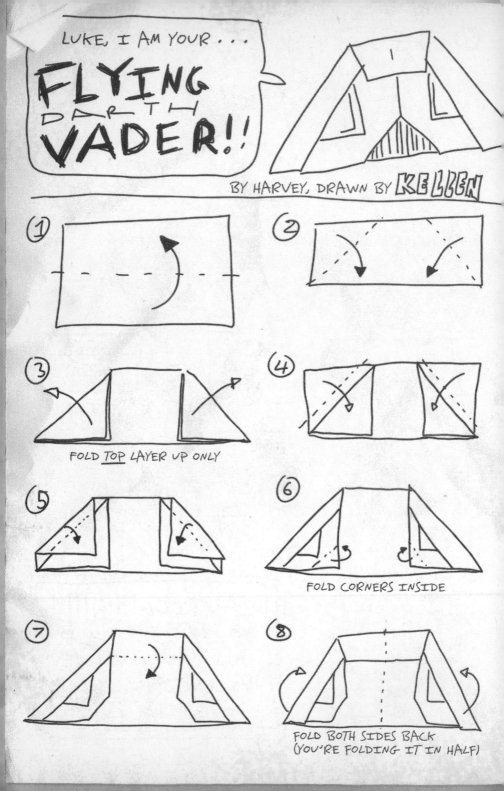

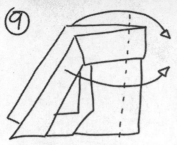

⑨

FOLD BOTH WINGS
FORWARD . . .

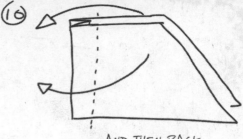

⑩

. . . AND THEN BACK
AGAIN ON A NEW LINE

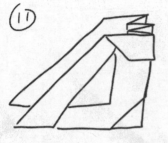

⑪

FOLD WINGS OUT FLAT,
LIKE THIS (SIDE VIEW)

W

DECORATE A BIT

⑫

IT'S (SORT OF) DARTH!!

AND FOR BETTER
FLIGHTS YOU MAY
WANT TO
"ADJUST THE
DIHEDRALS"
BY LIFTING THE
WINGS A BIT

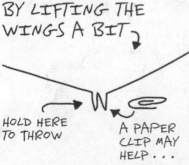

HOLD HERE
TO THROW

A PAPER
CLIP MAY
HELP . . .

⑬ THROW!!!

WHEEE!

CAUTION!!!!!!!!!!!!
DO **NOT** THROW IN
A MUSEUM FULL OF
PRICELESS HISTORICAL
ARTIFACTS!!!

ACKNOWLEDGMENTS

There are so many people who have contributed to this book and this series.

First there are the people who inspired this book, like George Lucas, Lawrence Kasdan, Tim Curry, Ian Diarmid, Dave Filoni, Matthew Wood, Brian Compton, Fumiaki Kawahata, and Eiji Nakamura.

Then the people who actually made the book happen, like Caryn Wiseman, Carol Roeder, Joanne Chan, Chad W. Beckerman, Susan Van Metre, Erica Finkel, Michael Jacobs, Melissa Arnst, Jim Armstrong, Jason Wells, Laura Mihalick, and Erica Warshal.

There are people who offer me endless support or are just awesome or both, like Linda Petzke, Barbara Bell, Cindy Minnick, Patti Rowland, Michael and Julia Hemphill, Mark Turetsky, and my parents, Wayne and Mary Ann Angleberger.

And there are many more . . . booksellers, bookreps, librarians, teachers, reading specialists, principals, the NerdyBookClub, and my author/illustrator buddies. I just couldn't have done this alone.

But now, I hope the adults will understand

if I give the rest of this space to the
SuperFolders: kids who sent in origami,
drawings, costumes, movies, and most of the
Star Wars snack jokes for Kellen's doodles.
Most importantly, they have shared their love
of *Star Wars* and origami and they inspired me
to keep writing these books.... and to finish
the series so they could find out how it ends.
   The SuperFolders....
   Ackbar, AgentYoda, Ahsoka, AhsokaTano,
Aiden,AJMCCraft, Alatariel, AlekzAndEr,
Alex, AlexanderTheGreat, AlexDarth99,
AmazingYoda, AnakinLuke, AnakinSkypaper,
ARCFives, Ar2D2, Art2D2, Art2D2Artist,
Art2MinecraftMan, AustinM, AwesomeEwok,
AwesomeGuy0, Awesome11223344, AwesomeJawa
   BaconFolder, Ben, BobaFold, BobDiggidy,
Bolt, Bruno
   C3P01, CPHP, CadFold, Cammy,
CaptainAwesome, CathleenK, CaveSpider10,
CB, CJ, Chewie101, Chewy14, Chewy17,
ChiefEwokLabelMaker, Chikinnn,
ChippySlusher, Clawgami56, Clone, CocoaBean,
Collecter, CoolDude167, CommanderCody107,
CommanderDiamonds225, ConnorR, Copyright66,
Crazo20000, Crisredhat
   Dan, DarkinVader, DarkPalkia, DarthCal,
DarthCaleb13, DarthFoldius, DarthJasm,

DarthJawa, DarthMaul89, DarthNoah,
DarthOrigami, DarthP, DarthScissorus,
DarthShredder, DarthYoda1717, DarthVaper,
DavidTheJedi, Deadpool2325, DeathStar100,
Delta4ce, DiegoChina, DJTheDog, Dman,
DroidStarFighter, DuncanSkyFolder, Dwight
    E210, Echo, EdTheBrit, Edwin, Eli2,
Elliota380, Embo, EmperorGonkDroid, EpicBoy,
EpicOrigamiMan, EthanDear, EvangamiYodana,
EvanR, EvilFoldyWan, EvilJawa,
EwoksAreAwesome, EwoksAreEpic, Ewok, Ewok03,
EwokFolder531
    Felix, FerociousApplesauce,
FoldedShinobi, FolderDude27,
Foldawan, FoldoFett, FoldingTrooper,
FoldOrigamiAlliance, FoldyWan, FoolOfATook,
FrancisYodaGuy
    Gaines, Galem88, Gandalf, Gavin,
GeneralGrievous, Ghostbuster, Gial,
Gid, Grant, GravityDefyer, Grievous,
Griffenhammer, Griffolder, GusGrissom
    Han, Hansel, Harald, Hayden,
HaydenSkywalker, Hexagon, HG, Hulk,
HyperSpaceChewy
    IfoldStuff, IloveStarWars,
IluvOrigamiYoda, ImperialGuard, Isabella,
    JabbaTheFett, JabbaThePuppett,
JabbazPuppet, Jack, JackGolden, Jackowan,
JackT, JacobFoldwalker, JangoFett,

JangoFett37, JangoFolder5, JarJar99,
JarJarDude, JasonXWing, Jawa345, JC,
JediCouncilMember, JediDoodler,JediJoey,
JediJutus, JediKnight1234, JediMaster1,
JediMattKenobi, JediTrevor, JediWiseSebby,
Jeff, Jeongr1, JellyBelly0414, Jeongr1,
Jessenia, JC, JG, Jgolumbia, JLSuperFolder,
JF0712, JKOrigami, Joshua, JuanA,
Judoippon, JuliaCole, JumpingCactus
    KingJedi, KingJoel, KirigamiGirl
    LandoCalrissian96, LauraH, LegoCody,
LegoGabe, LegoJabba4, Leopard207,
LexiStarWars, Liam, Light&Dark,
Lizzy266, LoganB, Lou, Lucawampa, Luke,
LukeSkyfolder18, LukeSkyfolder221,
LukeVader, LuluTheJedi
    MaceWindu111116, MaceWindu17, MagicMan,
Malak, Mandomaker, Mario4Fan, MassivelyMace,
Master, MasterFolder, MasterMax,
MasterOfTheCrease, MATH, MattSwuared87,
MattWeb2000, Matthewb, MayTheFoldBeWithYu27,
Maximus, MaxReboKeys, Mega3, Megabuster,
MeganPhred, Michael, MichaelGorFoldo,
Minecraft, Moochman, MrGreenWookiee,
MrWookieeA299, MudFlapper, MyrMyr, Mystery
    Nathanation, Neb, Nick05, Nick2627,
Nick555533, NickTheNotSoGreat, NinJedi, NoahV
    O_Yoda, ObiJohnKenobi, ObiKalebKenobi,
ObiWanKfoldy, OdeYoda, OKOrigami,

OrigamiBulbasaur, OrigamiCaptainRex,
OrigamiCdHelps, OrigamiJawa, OrigamiJedi,
OrigamiJediMaster, OrigamiMan1234,
OrigamiMatthew, OrigamiMe, OrigamiPadawan,
OrigamiSeb, OrigamiWarrior87, OrigamiYoda10,
OY217, Ozigami

   PacBat, PaperDragon, PaperLuigi,
Patten117, PauseenP, PercyJackson, Pi,
PloKoon23, PloKoon101, PokeFolder2003,
Posiedon, Princess, PrincessElla,
Proromayev, PurseGirl

   QuiFoldCrease, QuiGonJack, QuiGonJoe

   RadicalTrack97, Rancorman,
RainbowLightsaber, Ramazama2,
RealRedFrostSpike, Reproman, RexTheGreat,
RexMaximus, R2D2C3PO, R2DMo, RibBQ, RobbieK,
Robby, RockHopper, RyanR

   SalaciousCrumb, Salon9, Samy,
SaraLoves2Read, SeanSolo&Carson,
SebasTheFolder910, SEEDFolder, SFMGS01,
SFOmer, ShaakTi77, SithCollin, Sherlock,
SkyVader10, Slappy, SlickSkillet,
SnoopyGirl11, SnowAngel, Sonic12012,
Sonigami, Spence, SpiderMan777, Spike
1214, Spyrise, SpyTrooper101, StarWars101,
StarWarsYoda, StickFigureStudios, Sting251,
StookyJediYoda, StookyLukey, StookyMan100,
StookyMaster, StookyNate95, StookyYoda787,
StormTrooper, Superfolderethfan,

SuperMan, SuperStookynessMan, SuperYodaMan,
SWF12
   Tanner, TaunTaun, TedComic,
TheFoldIsWithYou, TheChosen1, TheYoda,
ThunderKicker, Tonigami, TMac13, Tyler,
TynamonZ
   Ultimate, UltraMaul, Unicorn, Vader,
VanJahnke
   Wiztron, WookieeFan, WookieeWolf,
Wooktent,
   Xcalibur, XYZ,
   Yoda565, Yoda8, Yodabird,YodaFett,
YodaForce, Yodamaster, YodaMaster223,YodaSF,
YodaTheGreat, YodarGreg
   Zack, Zod

   I especially want to thank all the
SuperFolders on the Jedi Council and all the
SFs who've been listed in previous books. And
any that I've missed. And all those who WILL
become SuperFolders soon!
   And, of course, I have to thank Origami
Yoda himself. He changed my whole life, after
all.
   Finally . . . I thank everybody who has
joined me for this story. I've had so much
fun telling it and I hope you've enjoyed
reading it.
   May the Force be with you . . . always.

ABOUT THE AUTHOR

Tom Angleberger is the author of the *New York Times* bestselling Origami Yoda series. He is also the author of *Fake Mustache* and *Horton Halfpott*, both Edgar Award nominees, and The Qwikpick Papers. Tom maintains the Origami Yoda–inspired blog origamiyoda.com. He is married to author-illustrator Cece Bell and lives in Christiansburg, Virginia.

This book was designed by Melissa J. Arnst and art directed by Chad W. Beckerman. The main text is set in 10-point Lucida Sans Typewriter. The display typeface is ERASER. Tommy's comments are set in Kienan, and Harvey's comments are set in Good Dog. The hand lettering on the cover was done by Jason Rosenstock.